"You ...sband
and kids," Justin ...er,
his grin mischievous.

"My *what?*" Patsy shrieked.

"Your...uh, talented and gifted kids." Justin bit
back a laugh.

Eyes narrowed, Patsy glared at him. He was
enjoying this. "You sent in my high school reunion
response that was supposed to be thrown away.
And you did it on purpose!"

"No! I didn't. Honest."

Patsy collapsed on the couch with a cry. "Where in
the *world,*" she muttered brokenly, "am I going to
get a *husband* and two talented and gifted *children*
in less than a month?" Slowly pulling herself up,
her gaze settled on Justin.

And his face fell.

Dear Reader,

Happy Holidays! Our gift to you is all the very best Romance has to offer, starting with *A Kiss, a Kid and a Mistletoe Bride* by RITA-Award winning author Lindsay Longford. In this VIRGIN BRIDES title, when a single dad returns home at Christmas, he encounters the golden girl he'd fallen for one magical night a lifetime ago. Can his kiss—and his kid—win her heart and make her a mistletoe mom?

Rising star Susan Meier continues her TEXAS FAMILY TIES miniseries with *Guess What? We're Married!* And no one is more shocked than the amnesiac bride in this sexy, surprising story! In *The Rich Gal's Rented Groom,* the next sparkling installment of Carolyn Zane's THE BRUBAKER BRIDES, a rugged ranch hand poses as Patsy Brubaker's husband at her ten-year high school reunion. But this gal voted Most Likely To Succeed won't rest till she wins her counterfeit hubby's heart! BUNDLES OF JOY meets BACHELOR GULCH in a fairy-tale romance by beloved author Sandra Steffen. When a shy beauty is about to accept *another* man's proposal, her true-blue *true* love returns to town, bearing *Burke's Christmas Surprise.*

Who wouldn't want to be *Stranded with a Tall, Dark Stranger*— especially an embittered ex-cop in need of a good woman's love? Laura Anthony's tale of transformation is perfect for the holidays! And speaking of transformations... Hayley Gardner weaves an adorable, uplifting tale of a Grinch-like hero who becomes a Santa Claus daddy when he receives *A Baby in His Stocking.*

And in the New Year, look for our fabulous new promotion FAMILY MATTERS and Romance's first-ever six-book continuity series, LOVING THE BOSS, in which office romance leads six friends down the aisle.

Happy Holidays!

Mary-Theresa Hussey
Senior Editor, Silhouette Romance

Please address questions and book requests to:
Silhouette Reader Service
U.S.: 3010 Walden Ave., P.O. Box 1325, Buffalo, NY 14269
Canadian: P.O. Box 609, Fort Erie, Ont. L2A 5X3

THE RICH GAL'S
RENTED GROOM

Carolyn Zane

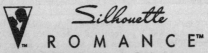

Silhouette
R O M A N C E™
Published by Silhouette Books
America's Publisher of Contemporary Romance

For Shawna Olds, a dear high school friend
who always makes me feel like a kid again.
THANK YOU
Dear Lord, for old friends and times of reunion.

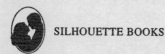

SILHOUETTE BOOKS

ISBN 0-373-19339-4

THE RICH GAL'S RENTED GROOM

Copyright © 1998 by Carolyn Suzanne Pizzuti

All rights reserved. Except for use in any review, the reproduction or utilization of this work in whole or in part in any form by any electronic, mechanical or other means, now known or hereafter invented, including xerography, photocopying and recording, or in any information storage or retrieval system, is forbidden without the written permission of the editorial office, Silhouette Books, 300 East 42nd Street, New York, NY 10017 U.S.A.

All characters in this book have no existence outside the imagination of the author and have no relation whatsoever to anyone bearing the same name or names. They are not even distantly inspired by any individual known or unknown to the author, and all incidents are pure invention.

This edition published by arrangement with Harlequin Books S.A.

® and TM are trademarks of Harlequin Books S.A., used under license. Trademarks indicated with ® are registered in the United States Patent and Trademark Office, the Canadian Trade Marks Office and in other countries.

Printed in U.S.A.

CAROLYN ZANE

lives with her husband, Matt, and her preschool daughter, Madeline, in the scenic rolling countryside near Portland, Oregon's Willamette River. Like Chevy Chase's character in the movie *Funny Farm*, Carolyn finally decided to trade in a decade of city dwelling and producing local television commercials for the quaint country life of a novelist. And, even though they have bitten off decidedly more than they can chew in the remodeling of their hundred-year-plus-old farmhouse, life is somewhat saner for her than for poor Chevy. The neighbors are friendly, the mail carrier actually stops at the box, and the dog, Bob Barker, sticks close to home.

THE BRUBAKER FAMILY
of Texas

Big Daddy - m. - Miss Clarise

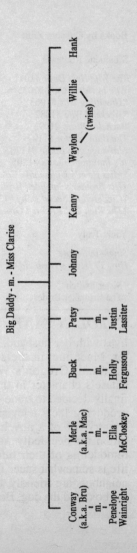

- Conway (a.k.a. Bru) — m. — Penelope Wainright
- Merle (a.k.a. Mac) — m. — Ella McCloskey
- Buck — m. — Holly Fergusson
- Patsy — m. — Justin Lassiter
- Johnny
- Kenny
- Waylon ⎫ (twins)
- Willie ⎭
- Hank

Chapter One

"Patsy, darlin'..." Big Daddy Brubaker, the diminutive patriarch of the large Brubaker clan, poked an expensive cigar into the corner of his rubbery lips. Then, settling back and folding his stubby hands across his middle, he eyed her with his sharp, raisinlike gaze. "...you just had a birthday, didn't you, honey pie?"

Patsy winced and nodded.

"Whatcha gonna be, sweet girl? Twenty-two? Twenty-three?"

"Twenty-eight."

"Twenty-*eight!*" he exploded, his face agog with wonder. "When the devil did *that* happen?" Big Daddy's voice was disgruntled as he stared at her. "Musta slipped my mind that you got a little older while you were abroad takin' them fancy dance lessons." He was thoughtful for a moment as he contemplated this new revelation. "Twenty-eight? Twenty*eeee*—" his sigh was heavy "—*aaaaaeeee*eight. And you're still livin' at home?" He shot a glance at his wife of so many years, Miss Clarise, and frowned.

"Yes, Big Daddy." Patsy shrugged, an expression of dismay marring her brow. She was no happier about the situation than he was.

To avoid the scrutiny in his gaze, she allowed her eyes to sweep the house that had been her home for her entire life, with the exception of the five years she spent studying dance in Europe.

It was a beautiful estate. The huge Brubaker antebellum mansion was breathtaking in both its style and enormity. Pillars, like sturdy sentinels, guarded the house proper, supporting what looked like acres of veranda on the first and second floors. The long driveway was lined with shade trees and a half dozen other buildings dotted the surrounding area. From where she sat, Patsy could see the servants' quarters, a giant garage, the pool house, a gazebo, a greenhouse, the professionally manicured rose gardens and the stables.

It was perfect except for one fact.

She should have been sitting in her own dining room, hosting her own Sunday brunch, with her own friends and family, she thought, nibbling her lower lip. Too bad she didn't have any. With the exception of her parents and siblings, Patsy had had little contact with the outside world of late.

She was tired. Weary. Depressed. Five years of studying dance in Europe, and what did she have to show for it? A few commercial gigs in Dallas to showcase her talents, and a bedroom suite in her father's house. She'd considered moving away again and trying to kick-start a flagging career in the highly competitive field of dance, but at this late stage of the game, what chance did she have? Not to mention, that after five years away from her parents and eight rowdy brothers, the idea of heading off to parts unknown held little appeal. In the five years she'd been overseas, she'd missed her three older brothers' weddings, and the birth of their babies.

A long, tired sigh puffed her cheeks and escaped her lips. Why must she be such a late bloomer when it came to figuring out what she wanted to be when she grew up? she mused, squirming under her father's burning gaze. Why hadn't she ever taken time to consider that there might not be that much opportunity to use a dance major and still live anywhere near her family? And beginning a dance career at the ripe old age of twenty-eight? Ha! She'd have laughed out loud, if it hadn't been so pathetic. Her passion for a lifetime of dance had disappeared somewhere along the way back in Europe, but she'd been too strong-willed to admit it.

She'd screwed up. Big time.

And hiding out at her father's pool and going soft for the last year wasn't helping matters. Restless and out of shape, Patsy knew she needed to get on with her life. Gripping the arms of her chair, she braced herself for the inevitable lecture from her father.

Big Daddy cleared his throat. "Darlin'..." he began, sitting forward and jerking the cigar out of the corner of his mouth and using it to stab at the air. "When was the last time y'all did somethin' with all those dance lessons I bought ya?"

"What do you mean?" Patsy feigned ignorance, as her mind groped for an answer where there was none.

"Wall, I paid for a bunch of schoolin' and I want to know what you intend to do with it. So far, you've managed to spend the last year making a career out of floatin' in the pool..."

Patsy squinted in shame at her hands. So, she thought miserably, he'd noticed.

"...and feelin' sorry for yourself and gainin' weight..."

"Wha...what?" Patsy sputtered, knowing full well her

father was referring to the ten extra pounds that had settled here and there on her frame, making it hard to zip up her dresses.

"Don't get me wrong, darlin', on you it looks good. But I'm just wondering when you're evah gonna get out of that pool and get on with your life."

"I've been *resting!*" she claimed, her tone defensive.

"Restin'? For a *year?*"

"You don't know what I've been through!" She hated the way she let him get under her skin.

"I've seen the credit card receipts, baby doll! Shoppin', tourin', winin' and dinin' don't take that much energy. I don't know what-all you were up to, over there in Europe, and…hup…wall…that's all in the past. But I'm tellin' ya here and now that it's time for you to get up off your chubby little duff and dance for your supper. Make it on your own, like your older brothers."

Patsy gasped. *Chubby little duff!* Of all the nerve!

"Why…why…" she sputtered, insulted, but knowing he was right. Her brothers were all hardworking men. They put her to shame.

Big Daddy's brow knotted into a mass of wrinkles. "Why, your older brothers are all married and have children of their own. Thriving careers and busy lives. You, on the other hand, have been out of high school for what? Hmm, now, good heavens." He calculated on his fingers. "*Ten* years now with nothing to show for yourself."

Patsy shifted uncomfortably in her chair.

"No husband, no children, no career. And in high school, *you* were the one voted most likely to succeed!" He snorted and his face glowed red as he geared up for yet another of his famous lectures to his offspring. As much as he preferred to coddle her, it was obvious that Big Daddy had decided that it was time for her to grow up.

"Big Daddy," Miss Clarise murmured, trying to placate

her husband before he said something he would inevitably regret. "I'm sure Patsy worked very hard in dancing school, and that she is a wonderful dancer now." She turned her silvering head toward her daughter. "Isn't that right, honey?"

Patsy couldn't lie. She hadn't worked hard. She'd shopped. She'd played. She'd toured. She'd spent five years being a spoiled brat. No, she couldn't lie, so she changed the subject.

"I'm perfectly capable of taking care of myself, Big Daddy!" she declared, vehemently. "And I'm also perfectly capable of...getting off my...my...*big fat fanny* and...and...dancing for my supper!" she shouted as she rose with her temper and slammed her fist on the table. Her younger siblings were all staring from the far end of the table, enjoying the show.

"Oh, sweetheart," Miss Clarise placated, patting her daughter on her arm. "We think you look beautiful just as you are. Don't we, Big Daddy? Tell her that she's not fat."

"Not yet she's not," Big Daddy roared, "but give her another year in the pool, and I'll be able to charge admission." He grinned at that one, knowing he was pushing her buttons. He hated to do it, but Patsy needed a little nudge in the right direction. It had worked with her brothers, it might work with her. "That will help defray some of the costs of her chow."

That did it. That was the straw that broke the dancer's back.

Cheeks flaming, Patsy pushed back her chair and spun to face her father. "I don't need your money. I'm perfectly capable of making my own way in this world!"

"Prove it!" Big Daddy challenged, gleefully rubbing his hands together. He loved to see the independent streaks come out in his children. "Get out there and find yourself a job. And, while you're at it, why don't you work on gettin' yourself hitched to some nice boy, and give your mama and me some grandkids?''

"*Augghhh!*" A guttural growl rumbled past Patsy's tightly clenched teeth.

To Big Daddy Brubaker, nothing was more sacred than family. That's why it was so important to him that each of his offspring find the love and happiness that he'd found with Miss Clarise. He had nine children in all; Conway, who had always answered to "Bru," Merle, whom everyone had dubbed "Mac," Buck, Patsy, Johnny, Kenny, the twins, Waylon and Willie and last, but most certainly not least, young teenage Hank. Much to their eternal chagrin, he had insisted on naming all of his children for country music stars. For if there was one thing that Big Daddy enjoyed nearly as much as he enjoyed his family, it was country music.

However, country music aside, everything else in Big Daddy's life paled in comparison to the importance of his family. Including his billion-dollar bank account, his rambling antebellum mansion known as the Circle B.O. for Brubaker Oil, his thousands of acres of Texas ranch land, his half dozen Fortune 500 companies, or his many productive oil fields.

"Go on with you now, and...and—" dimples creased his pliant cheeks "*—show me the money!*" Big Daddy chortled, as his daughter's eyes blazed into his.

"Oh, now, Big Daddy," Miss Clarise murmured, ever the peacemaker.

"Oh, I'll *show* you, all right," Patsy shrieked, much to her younger brothers' delight. They clapped and mimicked her, only serving to incite her fury. "Consider me on my own! From this moment on, I don't want another red cent from you, Big Daddy! Ever! And, don't worry. I won't let the screen door hit my *enormous butt* on my way out!" Whirling on her heel, cheeks on fire with purpose, Patsy stormed to her room and slammed the double doors, the sound thundering throughout the mansion's cavernous halls.

"Patsy!" her mother had called, alarm filling her soft Southern drawl. "Big Daddy, do something!"

"Let her be," Big Daddy advised, puffing contentedly on his cigar. "She'll be fine. You know," he said thoughtfully, "that little gal has a lot more going for her than she gives herself credit for. But, she's a lot like me. I think a dose of reality might be just what the doctor ordered to get her workin' hard."

Up in her room, Patsy hastily tossed a few belongings into a suitcase, emptied the wads of petty cash from her piggy bank into her purse and called a cab to meet her at the front gate before noon that day.

That was a week ago.

Patsy now lived in a cramped one-bedroom apartment on the poor side of Hidden Valley, Texas—not too far from Big Daddy's land—and was driving a gas-guzzling wreck of a giant old station wagon that she wouldn't have been caught dead in last month.

And now, here she was applying for a job with her sister-in-law, for the low paying position of receptionist for the Miracle House Ranch for orphaned children, just outside the little town of Hidden Valley.

She had made up her mind that she would not use her family's name to influence anyone into giving her a prestigious job that she didn't really deserve. And, Lord knew that Miracle House was anything but prestigious. Luckily, with as much secretarial training that she'd suffered through in high school, she was certainly qualified to handle this meager position. Couple that with the fact that no one else had applied—no doubt the paltry salary they were able to offer—and the job was practically hers.

Yes, Patsy thought, opening her eyes as the heavily pregnant, ever smiling Gayle trundled back into the room, she would earn her own way in this world. She would show Big Daddy. He wasn't the only one who could pull himself up from the depths of poverty and achieve greatness…to start from nothing and make a world-renowned name for himself. She could make her own way, thank you very much. Even starting here at the Miracle House.

If they would have her.

Gayle's youthful voice pulled her back to the stifling present.

"Miss Brubaker?"

"Yes?"

"Holly will see you now."

"Thank you." Wearily Patsy peeled herself away from her folding chair, and followed Gayle into Holly's office.

"Who is that?" Patsy casually gestured over her sister-in-law's shoulder with the application she still held in her hand.

In response to Patsy's question, Holly pushed slightly back from her desk and craned to see what was going on in the world past the small, aluminum window in her office.

"Oh, that's Justin Lassiter, our new ranch foreman."

Patsy's eyes followed his rangy gait as several kids skipped along beside him, eyes sparkling and jabbering a mile a minute. As he moved amid the throng of adoring children, Patsy couldn't help but stare. He had such an engaging grin, and he really seemed to be listening to the boy at his side. And handsome? What was he doing out here in the middle of nowhere talking to a bunch of grimy-faced kids, when he could be living the high life on the cover of *Gentlemen's Quarterly*? It was beyond Patsy.

Holly continued. "He's in charge of the horse program, organizes the riding lessons, teaches horse care, et cetera…right here at Miracle House Ranch. And what a godsend.'' An angelic smile tipped Holly's lips as she slowly shook her head. "Nobody understands the kids like Justin.''

"Really?'' Patsy queried, her gaze straining after the little troop as they disappeared into the stables.

"Mmm-hmm.'' Holly dropped forward, elbows to the desk and thoughtfully regarded Patsy. "He was once an orphan himself. Spent half his life in foster homes, some of 'em ranches. Then he eventually ended up working at Miracle House of Oklahoma City himself. He and I worked together for a number of years before Buck persuaded him to come use his horse talents out here on the ranch.''

"Hmm.'' Patsy still thought he should have gone for the career in modeling. Justin Lassiter, sporting a trendy pair of briefs, smiling at her from a billboard or magazine would definitely put the zing in her morning.

Cradling her cheek in her hand, Holly gazed at Patsy. "He's living proof that someone can pull themselves up from the depths of poverty and despair and make something of their life.''

Patsy blanched slightly, and refocused on her application. "Yes…well…'' She groped for something to say. Her sister-in-law's compassionate eyes told her that she knew Patsy was having a tough time of it these days. Chagrined, Patsy smoothed her hair back into her sagging chignon, and tried to appear more poised and sophisticated than she felt.

Tapping her pencil lightly on her blotter, Holly glanced out the window, a faraway look in her eyes. "I've always wished Justin had a family of his own.''

"He's not married?'' Patsy wondered, morbid curiosity forcing the question from her lips. Not that she really cared one way or another. Obviously she and Justin were from completely different worlds. Patsy went for the dashing, sophisticated, European man, with the bottomless pocketbook. A small smile tinged her lips at the memory of her

handsome playboy buddy, Henri and his endless—and in-
famous—yacht parties.

Even so, she had to admit she'd never laid eyes on any
man so compelling as Justin Lassiter.

"Oh, no. Justin has been hurt very badly in his life. He's
very wary of intimate relationships of any kind. If you
knew his history, you'd understand. It's too bad, though,"
Holly mused, "he's such a good man. He ought to get
married and have some kids of his own. He would make
such a wonderful father."

Patsy's laughter reverberated off the hollow trailer pan-
eling. "You think everyone would make a wonderful father
since you got pregnant."

Lashes dropping, Holly smiled proudly at her rounding
midsection. "True. Still," she insisted, "Justin would make
some poor kid a nice dad. Too bad he's so gun-shy." Holly
went on to regale Patsy with a few tidbits about Justin's
brief engagement to a woman named Darlene.

"Mmm," Patsy absently agreed, smoothing her application form out on Holly's desk. At the moment, she was
more concerned about her own future than Justin's.

For the better part of an hour, the two women discussed
the job opening. Holly outlined the various duties of the
receptionist, and did her best to sell Patsy on the idea of
working for her brother Buck. There were several things
Patsy hadn't anticipated as duties, such as helping with the
annual fund-raiser, but with a halfhearted shrug, she decided that she was game. Holly also suggested that Patsy
might consider helping out with some dance lessons for the
kids.

"With your talent and extensive study, I'm sure you
could teach a wonderful series of courses in dance, Patsy!"
Holly enthused. "Remember, back when we were kids,
how we'd put on those ballets for our folks?"

Patsy smiled. She remembered. Those times were some

of her fondest memories as a child. She'd always believed that someday she would be a world-famous ballerina. However, as she'd gotten older, she began to realize that she didn't have what it took. Not really. Oh, she was good. But not great. And certainly not dedicated enough to make it to the big time. A beleaguered sigh had Patsy sagging into her chair. Teaching dance to homeless children and playing part-time receptionist certainly wasn't what she'd envisioned doing with her life, but it would tide her over in a pinch.

"Okay," she said, her dismal exhalation speaking more of a trip to the gallows than of a new position at Miracle House. "I'll take it."

"Oh, wonderful!" Holly cried, her eyes gleaming. "You can start first thing in the morning. I'll have Gayle clean out that desk in the entry area for you."

The distant lyrics of an old song flitted through Patsy's brain. She would survive, she thought, a sudden surge of adrenaline lifting her out of her chair to thrust her hand at her sister-in-law to seal the deal. Yes. It was no small accident that she'd been voted most likely to succeed by her high school graduating class.

Big Daddy was not the only one who could pull off the rags-to-riches story, she thought, a smug grin gracing her lips as she bid Holly goodbye and strode purposefully out of the trailer toward her newly purchased, dirt-cheap, giant, dust-covered, wood-paneled station wagon. Sliding over the protruding springs, she thrust the key into the engine, and enthusiastically pumped the gas pedal. All she needed now was a little soak in her rust-ringed bathtub, and some shut-eye on her lumpy futon, and she'd be off to the races to begin her new life, bright and early in the morning.

If her car ever decided to start.

Chapter Two

Two months later, Patsy Brubaker pressed her face to the window just above her wobbly, battle-scarred desk, in the less than miraculous lobby of the Miracle House Ranch's main office.

"Have mercy," she groaned against the glass.

Flattening her cheek and nose against the dusty pane, she rolled her face to better watch the half-naked Greek god—who went by the mortal name of Justin Lassiter—flash across the rolling pasture in the late autumn Texas heat. Long legs pumping, muscles bulging, sweat glistening, teeth sparkling, he was a rare sight to behold, indeed.

Just like some kind of darned superhero, Patsy thought grumpily as she watched him leap into the air—reach for the football as it spiraled its way toward him—and effortlessly trap it in his perfectly sculpted hands. With the exception of the older girls, who wore swimsuit tops, everyone was shirtless and cutoff jeans were the order of the day. Old sneakers and white socks graced everyone's feet. Shaking his dark, shaggy, sweat-soaked hair out of his eyes,

Justin listened to what one of the older, and considerably well-developed, girls had to say, threw his head back and let loose with a peal of laughter that served only to further irritate Patsy.

It was hard to pinpoint exactly what it was about Justin Lassiter that ruffled her buttons and pushed her feathers this way. Sighing, she lifted the damp tendrils of hair from the back of her neck and wearily fanned herself with her hand. After all, she mused—shelving her bad mood for a moment in order to allow a charitable thought—it wasn't his fault that he was a devastatingly handsome man. Or that he had a fantastic sense of humor. Or that women everywhere seemed to find him irresistible. Perhaps a lot of her agitation with Justin stemmed from the fact that he didn't seem to notice that she was alive.

He treated her like a kid sister. A pesky one at that.

Her, of all people. Patsy Brubaker. Socialite. Educated. Manicured. Sister of the boss. Attractive in spite of the ten extra pounds she carried. Nine pounds, actually. She couldn't afford lunch anymore. Touching her pursed lips with the tip of her tongue, she bristled. Patsy was not used to being ignored by the men in her life. Ever since she was a baby, males of all ages had fawned over her.

Everyone but Justin Lassiter, it seemed. In fact, if she didn't know better, she would swear that Justin didn't even like her. What was that all about? What the heck had she ever done to him? Well, she didn't care. She would just ignore him. But it was hard. He seemed to be everywhere at the ranch, always in on the meetings, always needing her to retrieve things from the files, write letters, make calls and coffee. And never once had he given her more than a cursory, politically correct glance. His arrogant attitude bugged her. After all, it wasn't as if he was…well, as if he was…anybody.

No, Justin, she thought, her breath quickening slightly as

she watched his fluid movement—and Patsy always noticed fluid, graceful movement—was a creature of a different stamp. He was a fully grown, fully independent, fully self-contained…man.

With an easy agility, Justin backed up several paces, took aim and fired the ball back to the other side of the yard, where Patsy's older brother, Buck, along with a gaggle of hollering and jumping kids, stood waiting. Lolling on the window, she watched in amazement as the guys, and of course the kids, zigged and zagged around Holly's flower beds, leaping and bounding, throwing and catching, laughing and shouting as if the sweltering humidity were nothing more than a delightful, breezy spring afternoon, instead of an autumn heat wave. For pity's sake. Thanksgiving was right around the corner. Surely the heat should be letting up soon. Still no air conditioning in the budget, and in the afternoon hours, the little trailer became a veritable furnace.

Giggling teenage girls preened and posed more than they played. Patsy couldn't really blame them. The two men, who had so enthusiastically led the trampling of Holly's flower beds, were both gorgeous. And, had it been twenty or so degrees cooler, she might have been tempted to go out and join the mayhem.

Unfortunately she was too hot and grumpy. She blew at her wispy bangs and stared at the ever-growing pile in her In-basket. How was she ever supposed to keep up? Especially with Adonis streaking around just outside the window to constantly distract her. Late-autumn sunlight backlit Justin as he shook the hair from his eyes and planted his hands on his narrow hips. For a moment, his gaze flitted to hers, as if he could feel her stare, then bounced away. On to more interesting things, Patsy thought churlishly.

Exasperated, she focused on the clutter that covered her desk, and rubbed her temples.

The noise. The heat. The drudgery of her duties.

She should have known this would never work. The nine-to-five grind just didn't sit well with her artistic nature. Oh well, she sighed, things being what they were for her, she would just have to grin and bear it for a little while longer. Couldn't buy groceries with an artistic nature. Couldn't go crawling back to Big Daddy.

Better get back to work.

Doggedly she slogged though her mountainous In-basket, answering this thing, sorting and filing those things, paying that thing and calling back on the other thing. When she wasn't digging herself out from under the paper chase, she answered the phone.

"Miracle House Ranch. Patsy speaking. May I help you?" She felt like a broken record.

From time to time, her eyes strayed out the window to Justin, and followed his broad pectoral muscles, flexing and bouncing as he jogged backward and twirled the pigskin between his fingertips.

Fantasies of Justin and herself stranded on a not so deserted island filled her mind. A mariachi band played softly in the background, palm fronds bobbed in the cool breezes, and Justin—gazing adoringly at her as the cabana boy freshened her drink—reached out, cupped her cheek, his perfectly sculpted lips forming her name… *Patsy… Oh… Patsy, how could I have been so blind…?*

Her reverie was broken by the daily arrival of the Hidden Valley mail carrier.

Beep! Beep!

The mailman leaned on his horn, announcing his arrival as he drove onto the fifty-yard line of the impromptu football game. Hopping out of his van, the mail carrier, deciding to join in on the fun, rushed across the pasture and smoothly handed off today's mail bundle to Buck.

Tucking the bundle under his arm, Buck ran to the driveway, darted a quick glance at the playing field, then motioned for Justin to drop back to the area near the paddock for a pass. Unable to resist the challenge, Justin ran backward, eyes up, head moving, trying to catch the mail missile that exploded midair into a fluttering, flapping, scattergun pile of paper, most of which landed in a pile of manure.

This of course, only served to further frustrate the already hot and bothered Patsy. Leaping from her chair, she yanked open the front door.

"Thanks a lot, you big boobs," she huffed as she rushed out into the sweltering heat, picking her way past the sloppier manure piles to gather the soiled mail.

The mailman wisely disappeared in a cloud of dust.

"How on earth am I supposed to read this?" she shrieked into Justin's grinning face, then, hating herself for the fishwife she was portraying, turned to share her ill-humor with her laughing brother. "Don't you guys have some work to do?" She knew she was coming off like a first-class shrew, but hot damn, she was boiling. And now this? Her eyes began to burn and her nose wrinkled at the wretched odor. Pinching the gamey and dripping stack of mail out in front of her at arm's length, Patsy stormed back into the trailer, muttering over her shoulder. "Thanks for nothing, you big clowns."

"Anytime, kiddo," came Justin's rakish reply, just before he was knocked flat by a cavalcade of kids.

Kiddo, Patsy sighed to herself and shoved the front door closed behind her. What would it take to get Justin Lassiter to stop seeing her merely as some kind of juvenile? At twenty-eight years old, she was hardly a kid by anyone's yardstick. Must be the fact that she was Buck's little sister.

Tossing the mail into the sink in the kitchenette, Patsy grabbed a damp dishcloth and did her best to clean off the stinky envelopes. Although, she suspected she'd be even more depressed when she finished her task. Most likely, it was just more work.

Work, work, work, and to make matters worse, the paltry salary she earned here, for all her slaving away, barely made ends meet. With a sigh, she bundled the dripping mess in a stack of paper towels and carted it to her desk.

Justin watched as Patsy—her cute gamin face puckered into a disgusted scowl, her deep blue eyes snapping—sashayed back into the office trailer and slammed the door behind her.

What was stuck in her craw? he wondered, watching as the ever-present thundercloud that hovered above her beautiful, flaxen head was sucked into the office behind her. Justin shook his head and sighed in irritation. The boss's younger sister always seemed to have her nose out of joint about something.

Patsy was an unfortunate reminder of his ex-fiancée, Darlene. Beautiful, rich, spoiled rotten and sure that the planet rotated for her benefit alone. A long time ago, Justin had sworn off women like Darlene. Even working with someone who merely resembled Darlene gave him the heebiejeebies. And, unfortunately, working with Patsy was unavoidable. For now. Hopefully this situation was only short-term. Patsy didn't strike Justin as the usual working girl. She was too used to being pampered. He was surprised she'd lasted two months so far.

However, to be perfectly fair, she did have pretty decent phone skills. Since Patsy had come on board, he'd actually gotten his messages in a timely fashion. The coffee had improved considerably, too, he thought on a charitable whim. So, okay, maybe she wasn't all bad. She had a few redeeming characteristics. That's more than he could manage to find in Darlene these days.

He sighed.

Perhaps, until Patsy finally decided to throw in the towel,

he could tolerate her. After all, she was the sister of the boss.

It was just so irritating, the way he seemed to run into her every time he turned around. Company meetings, coffee and lunch breaks in the break room, the class-rooms...doggone it, *everywhere.* Justin raked a hand over his face as he trotted back out onto the playing field. Her perky upturned nose would likely drive him to distraction. What was it about her heart-shaped face and pouty rosebud mouth that had his head in such a dither so much of the time? For crying in the night, he didn't even *like* the woman.

Shaking his head to rid it of this destructive train of thought, Justin lifted his hands above his head, and flagged one of the boys on his team as the ball was put into play.

"Over here," he shouted, his head turning back and forth, his feet moving now in slow motion to carry his body into position to catch the spiraling ball. "I got it!" he heard himself shout, even as he could feel Patsy's eyes on him through the cracked pane of glass that separated her desk from the playing field.

A lapse in sanity had him turn his head slightly to catch her eye.

Yep.

There she was, watching him, the way Darlene used to watch him. Lashes lowered haughtily. Lips bowed into a tiny smile. Perfectly coiffed. Perfectly sophisticated. Perfectly spoiled. And, as cool as a cucumber even in this ungodly heat. Just like Darlene. It was eerie.

Man. Patsy was tempting. Tempting, in a horrible, I'll-hate-myself-in-the-morning kind of way. *Danger, Will Robinson,* a tiny voice in his brain shouted, as he stared at her fantastically beautiful face. *911! Come in Adam 12! She's the boss's sister! Alert! Alert! Remember demanding Darlene the debutante!*

Yeah. He'd learned the hard way that such different backgrounds didn't mix. He'd come from an orphanage. Before that, foster homes, and before that, the street.

He'd been to hell and back before he'd reached his teens.

He didn't need some spoiled rich girl to turn his head. To make him long for things best left alone.

Unable to turn his head from Patsy's entrancing gaze in time to catch the ball, Justin suddenly found himself flayed out, facedown, studying the stubbled wheat field's roots.

Tearing her eyes away from Justin's prone body out on the playing field, Patsy stabbed into yet another envelope with her letter opener. *Hmm,* she thought, her eyes scanning the postmark, then landing on the orange-and-black label. It had been forwarded to her at the ranch, from her mother. That's odd. Almost everyone had her new address now...

She scrubbed at the return address with a damp paper towel until the name of her high school alma mater appeared. A long forgotten—slightly off-key—rendition of the Willow Creek fight song flitted through her mind, squeaky tubas, thundering bass drums and all.

Willow Creek, our alma mater, hail to thee we sing...

"Oh, no," Patsy murmured as she tore open the envelope and discovered that her ten-year high school reunion was just over a month away. Smoothing out the soiled form, she stared at it in dismay. Had it really been ten years already? Good heavens, where had the time gone? Her eyes strayed to the attached page.

Oh and look. There was perky head cheerleader, Bitsy Hart's picture smiling cheerfully back at her from beneath the Willow Creek Alumni Association letterhead. Patsy grimaced. The terminally upbeat Bitsy *would* be in charge of the reunion. It didn't help matters that she looked like a million bucks, either, Patsy thought dismally, sucking in her stomach as she read the note.

Hi there, fellow alum!
Yes! Ten years have gone by and it's time to get together and find out what we've all been up to. Please take the time to fill out and send in the enclosed questionnaire. Bram and I have taken the liberty of filling out a sample for you to follow. Get the completed bio back to me as soon as possible, so that I can include it in the souvenir book that we will distribute at the reunion. Hope you all can attend! The reunion committee chose the days between Christmas and New Year's, hoping that the majority of you would be home for the holidays. See you in December!
Best Regards,
Bitsy Hart

Reunion Committee

Patsy sagged against her desk as her eyes scanned the bio on Bitsy and Bram's perfect life. They now lived in an exclusive section of Willow Creek, just south of Dallas, with their three perfect children, Barron, Brianna and Bryce. Bram owned his own business, Bitsy sold billions of dollars worth of real estate and for fun, they enjoyed yachting, golfing and touring the world. They were disgustingly successful. She knew she should be feeling proud and happy for them, but instead, a keen sense of failure settled deep in her gut.

Patsy sighed and stared at her blank questionnaire. *"Good grief,"* she muttered under her breath. This was just terrible. *She* had been the one voted "The Girl Most Likely to Succeed." A groan of despair rumbled deep in her throat. And just what, exactly, was the girl voted most likely to succeed supposed to write?

That she still hadn't made it all the way through college?

She cringed at the thought of all the money Big Daddy had wasted on her sporadically attended dance classes.

Cradling her head in her hands, Patsy shrugged against the knots in her neck. No, she hadn't obtained a degree, let alone a marriage certificate. And what should she write in the blank for children? Should she tell them that she now had twenty-five children, all orphans? That she currently worked as a temporary, in a grant-funded position, for her *brother,* no less? That she lived in a dump and drove one to boot? The panic began to rise beneath her breast.

No way.

She couldn't write *that*.

She'd sooner die.

No way was she going to give all her old classmates the satisfaction of reading the truth about her lackluster life. She could just hear everyone demanding a recount on the old "Most Likely to Succeed" vote.

Studying Bitsy's terminally perky smile, Patsy felt a sudden surge of defiance. Why should she feel obligated to explain to her old classmates why she didn't have a degree? Or a husband, or children, or an upwardly mobile career or...or even a pair of stockings that didn't have runs, for that matter?

Plus, she rationalized, it wasn't as if she was actually contemplating *going* to this stupid thing anyway. For heaven's sake, she hadn't kept up with any of these people. Why, she hadn't even spoken with any of her close friends in at least eight or nine years. Everyone had just seemed to drift apart.

An unwanted spark of curiosity flared to life in the back of her mind. She may not care about getting together with any of these people, but she couldn't help but wonder about them.

Were they all as successful as Bitsy and Bram? Thoughtfully she picked up a pencil and chewed the eraser tip as she stared unseeing out the window at the football game, still rollicking along despite the heat. She knew she should be a trooper and fill out the form, but she simply couldn't bring herself to admit the dismal truth.

The wheels slowly began to turn in the impish side of her mind.

Perhaps... Hmm, yes, *perhaps she should just make something up.* She giggled. As a joke. A prank. A little game. Yes. That would be fun. Give everyone a few laughs. Something so outlandish, most likely no one would ever really believe it, but something that would conceal the not so successful truth.

Yes, she thought, the mirth bubbling into her throat. This was a good idea. She would just dash off a little spoof of Bitsy and Bram's sample questionnaire. If anything, it should win her points as class clown.

Brow furrowed, Patsy touched the tip of her pencil to her tongue, then set to work feverishly filling in all the blanks, giggling here and guffawing there. Nobody in their right mind would ever believe a word of it. Minutes ticked by as she labored. So focused was she on her task that she did not hear Buck and Justin tromp into the trailer after the game, bringing with them a hot gust of wind and the scent of ripened athletes.

"Ah," Buck said with pride, striding over to Patsy's desk and ruffling her blond locks with his dirty hands, "just what I like to see, my employees hard at work."

Patsy reared away from his hand and smoothed her hair. Eyes squinting, nose wrinkled, she regarded the two. "*Eeewww.* Don't you guys have something better to do? Like shower for instance?"

"Nah," Buck growled, grabbing her in a bear hug and burying her face in his sweaty chest. "We just came in to make sure my favorite employee was happy as a clam."

"*Mffp, ack, pfff,*" came Patsy's muffled reply, as she

beat helplessly on her brother's arms. He rubbed the top of her head with the football, then released her and tucked the ball under his arm.

"Isn't that right, Justin?"

"Mmm." Justin nodded as he guzzled cold water from the sink tap. Wiping his mouth on the back of his hand, he sauntered over to join Buck and his sister at her desk.

"What are you working on now?" Buck wondered, looking over Patsy's head to the stack of paperwork on her desk.

"Nothing that concerns you," she snapped, nudging him out of her way.

"You hear that, Justin?" Buck asked, feigning wounded feelings. "And I own the place."

"She's a bossy little thing, isn't she?" Justin drawled, planting his hands on his hips.

His voice was low and just over her shoulder and like a spark sizzling along the fuse to a stick of dynamite, a riot of gooseflesh shot down her spine. Preferring to ignore him, Patsy refused to turn around and meet the probing emerald gaze she sensed in her peripheral vision. She could hear his breathing, still somewhat labored from his play, and knew that his sweaty, muscular, perfectly formed pectorals were no doubt heaving in a most fascinating, male animal kind of way. Closing her eyes against the temptation to look, she glared at her brother instead.

"What are you guys doing, besides trying to bug me?"

Buck shrugged. "Just wanted to see how you were doing before I went home to check on Holly's latest craving."

"Well, I'm fine," she chirped, "so you can get back to your pickles and ice cream now."

"Not so fast, now, sis. There's one more thing." Buck grabbed Justin and shoved him into the chair next to her desk. "We wanted to say we were sorry, right, bud?"

Justin nodded, a hangdog expression barely covering his

twitching lips. "Uh, yeah. Right. We're sorry." Valiantly he struggled to look contrite.

"For what?" Patsy demanded.

"For, uh—" Justin bit down on his lower lip and glanced up at Buck "—you know, dropping your mail in the...the..."

"Poop," Buck helpfully supplied.

Justin threw back his head and laughed.

Buck nudged him playfully. "So, sis, were you able to clean it off okay?"

Dragging a folding chair away from the wall to her desk, Buck dropped his lanky body into the seat he'd inserted between Justin and Patsy. Then he leaned forward, squeezing himself into the slot he'd created between their arms. As he peered over Patsy's shoulder, he began to paw through the stack of mail on her desk.

"Smells pretty good to me," Justin volunteered.

Buck paused as he came to the orange-and-black letterhead. "What's this?" he wondered.

Lazily Justin's eyes wandered from Patsy's face to Buck's hands.

"Nothing," she said as nonchalantly, in an effort to distract him. She had no desire to discuss her little practical joke with these two Bohemians.

Her brother's attention suddenly shot and riveted to the Willow Creek Alumni Association letterhead. "Say, isn't that Itsy-Bitsy Hart?" he asked, pointing to the reunion flyer. "Justin, get a load of Itsy-Bitsy, here."

Leaning across her brother, Justin peered at the flyer. Although the room was hideously hot, Patsy shivered as his breath tickled the hairs at the crook of her elbow. Criminy, this trailer was small. Why they were all practically sitting in each other's laps. As unobtrusively as she could, Patsy moved her arms across the nutty answers she'd scribbled in the blanks of the questionnaire Bitsy had enclosed with the flyer.

"So, what's the deal?" Buck wanted to know. "Why is Bitsy sending you this?"

"It's the notice for our ten-year class reunion." She leaned forward to more effectively hide what she'd written.

"Ten years?" Justin stared at her in surprise. "You've been out of high school for *ten* years?"

His tone of voice rankled. Made her feel about ten years old. "So?" Unable to stand his thorough scrutiny, she squirmed in her chair and studied her botched attempt at a home manicure and wished she'd taken a little time to run a comb through her hair. "What's your point?"

"Well," Justin said with a slight shrug, "it's just..."

"Just what?" she asked breezily, hoping she looked as if she couldn't care less about his opinion.

"It's just that you don't look old enough to have been out of high school ten years, that's all."

Pushing a curly golden lock away from her eyes, she glared at him, then at her brother. "When will you guys stop acting like Big Daddy and get it through your thick skulls that I'm not a little kid anymore? That I'm perfectly capable of taking care of myself. I'm an adult!" she insisted, realizing as she spoke that per usual, she'd thrown her tongue into gear before her brain. And she'd wanted so desperately to sit there in quiet dignity, proving her maturity to no one but herself. But, alas, it was too late. She was on a roll. "Just because Big Daddy thinks I'm going to come crawling home any minute, admitting defeat and begging him to take me in, doesn't make it so. I've changed over the past few months, being on my own and all."

The men exchanged amused glances.

"I *have!*" She narrowed her eyes at the two men. "I'm all grown up."

Patsy caught her lower lip between her teeth and felt her

cheeks grow even warmer than they already were, given the stifling temperature. That was the problem with being the only girl in an otherwise all-male family. She always felt as if she had something to prove.

I'm all grown up. She grimaced. What a stupid thing to say. Who was she trying to convince?

Justin's eyes dipped low for a moment, then slowly traveled up to meet her gaze. "True." The insolent word was loaded with innuendo. "You are all grown up."

As his gaze tangled and danced with hers, Patsy felt her heart pick up speed. If she didn't know better, she would be tempted to think that he was flirting with her. Her mouth went as dry as the dusty paddock just outside. No. Justin Lassiter didn't like her. He wouldn't flirt with her. A wave of goose bumps crashed against the shore of her spine as his gaze flicked lazily over her face and landed for a moment on her lips. Of their own volition, her eyes strayed to his mouth, and she wondered—in a moment of insanity—what it would be like if he leaned across Buck and over the desk and pressed those chiseled, soft, sexy lips to her own. Blinking away these images, Patsy cast her eyes back to her desktop and tried to bring her galloping heartbeat back to a mere trot.

Oblivious to the tense byplay between Justin and his sister, Buck slipped the bright orange bio questionnaire from beneath Patsy's elbow and scanned her answers.

"*Dr.* Patsy Brubaker?" Buck's eyes widened and he began to laugh. "*Astronaut?*"

"It's a joke," she sighed. Suddenly, under Justin's laughing eyes, it didn't seem so hilarious. "Give it to me," she ordered, holding out her hand.

Buck ignored her. "Hey, Justin," he hooted, "get a load of this! Did you know that sis works for NASA as a space shuttle pilot?"

Much to Patsy's flame-faced chagrin, Buck and Justin

proceeded to roar with laughter and—for what seemed like an eternity—tease her unmercifully over the answers she'd concocted. Pushing her lips into an irritated pucker, Patsy drummed her fingertips on the table and bristled.

Sobering for a moment, Justin looked hopefully at Patsy. "Next time you go to outer space, can I go, too?"

"Yeah, sis." Buck's tone was mocking. "I always wanted to take a ride in the space shuttle—" his gaze dropped back to the form that he held just out of Patsy's reach "—oh wait, before I go, do you think I could get your plastic surgeon husband to give me a tummy tuck?" To Justin he confided, "Ever since Holly got pregnant, I've sprouted love handles." He grabbed an inch of his firm belly for display purposes.

As he did so, Patsy snatched the questionnaire out of his hand and began to scrub at some of the blanks with an eraser.

"Okay," she conceded somewhat glumly. "Maybe astronaut was going a bit too far, but the rest of it is really good. Look here. The dancing part is true. Well," she amended as she erased all references to NASA, "some of the dancing stuff is true anyway. Besides. It's just a joke."

Stretching, Buck pushed his chair from between theirs, then, drawing himself to his feet, he ambled toward the kitchen looking for something to drink. Finding a can of soda, he hovered in the doorway and watched his sister try to wriggle out from Justin's pointed questions.

Justin had scooted over and was peering over Patsy's shoulder. "Why the phony answers? Why don't you just tell them the truth?"

Turning, Patsy lifted her lashes, her gaze stabbing him. "Why don't you go home?"

Shrugging, Justin's tone dripped with sarcasm. "Because I like it so much better up here with you in the mansion at Rolling Green Heights."

"Don't you recognize a practical joke when you see one?"

"Are you sure that's all it is?" Justin probed.

"Yes!"

"I think you are simply afraid to tell the truth." Bingo. Knowing he'd discovered a sore spot, Justin's brow arched critically.

Patsy fairly vibrated with irritation. She wanted to punch him in his perfectly tanned and toned guts. "I most certainly am not!"

"In that case, change all the answers and tell the truth."

"I most certainly will not!"

"Coward." The word was barely a whisper as it crossed Justin's lips.

Incensed, Patsy pointed to the door. "Go home."

Justin shrugged. "You are making a mistake, if you send that letter."

"I am not! I'll bet you wouldn't go around bragging to your high school class about that…that—" she pointed out the window at the bunk trailer across the way "—rolling tin can you call a home," she flung churlishly at him, then hated herself for the wounded look that briefly crossed his too handsome features. She might want to punch him in the guts, but she didn't really want to hurt his feelings.

Justin had been saving to build a house on a parcel of the ranch grounds he'd purchased next door to Buck and Holly's place. Patsy knew that. The trailer remark had been a low blow. Especially considering his unfortunate past.

"Now hold on just a minute," Justin growled, his eyes narrowing. "At least I'm not ashamed to admit that I live in a bunkhouse on a ranch for under…*privileged*—" he spat the word contemptuously "—children. I'm proud of what I do for a living. That I'm saving up to build a house. And, if I'd been lucky enough—" he pinned her to the back of her chair with scathing eyes "—to graduate with a class that threw fancy reunions, I'd tell 'em the truth on my little questionnaire." Jaw working, he leaned forward on his elbows and looked directly at her. "But I went to a public school that didn't think reunions were worth the time and effort, and then worked my way through college, earning *my* degree at *night*."

Pushing off the doorway, Buck guzzled the last of his soda, and burped pleasantly.

"Hey come on now—" he placated them, sensing something amiss in the air "—don't fight in front of the kids," he joked. At Justin's quizzical look, Buck pointed to the answers that Patsy had manufactured. "She has two kids. Talented and gifted."

Justin snorted. "So, Patsy, do you drop them off at school on your way to outer space every day?"

"Oh, blow it out your ear, Justin." She brandished the questionnaire in his smug, handsome face. "Read my lips. This…is…a…*joke*."

"No it's not. It's a cop-out."

"Oh sure." Her pursed mouth drew his gaze. "I suppose you want me to simply fill in my profession as Big Fat Failure." As she spoke, she viciously scrubbed out the last vestiges of her NASA profession, and prepared to print the truth.

Buck cleared his throat and ran a hand over his belly. "Hey, now, sis. I don't think of your working here as being a failure," he said and frowned. "This is a great place to work. Besides, you are doing just fine at your job. In a few more months, we might actually be able to give you a little raise."

"Okay! Okay! I give up. You guys win. I won't send it in, already." Crumpling the bio, she stuffed it into the return envelope and tossed it back into the overflowing In-basket.

"Good girl," Justin said. "You won't regret it."

Patsy's head dropped with a thud to the table. "You guys just don't get it."

"What's to get?" Justin wondered, thrusting an impatient hand through his satiny hair.

It was silent for so long that Justin feared she might not answer.

"I was voted 'The Girl Most Likely to Succeed.'" Her moans were muffled by the stacks of paperwork on her desk.

"Oh…" Justin said, a sudden—and somewhat cynical—understanding in his voice.

"Oh…" Buck said and shrugged, oblivious to his sister's angst. "Well, see ya in the morning guys. I gotta go check on Holly."

Chapter Three

The following Saturday found Patsy working overtime, yet again. Resting her fingertips on the keyboard of the ancient manual typewriter, she glanced up and smiled at the police officer as he entered the lobby of the Miracle House Ranch. It was all the project could do to stretch the grant money until the end of the year, hence, the lack of a computer. And the lack of decent office furniture. And a decent copier. And a decent coffee machine.

The list of needs was practically endless.

But Buck and Holly were optimistic. Money was coming at the first of the year, from various charitable sources. Big Daddy continued to pressure Buck and Holly to take his money, and the business advice that accompanied it, but both Buck and Holly were adamant about doing this project on their own. The pride in Big Daddy's eyes was unmistakable, when they'd turned down his generous offer.

"Hi, Officer. What can I do for you today?" Patsy asked as pleasantly as she could, given that quitting time was an hour ago. Pushing back her chair, she rose and, stepping to the front of her cluttered desk, poked her head out the customer service window into the darkly paneled waiting area. Her smile faded slightly as she spotted the two identical redheaded, freckle-faced troublemakers he had under each arm.

Marky and Mikey Flannigan. Two of the ranches most...challenging youths.

"These two tell me that they're supposed to spend their after-school hours here, working with their—" The officer cleared his throat, and leaned his straining belt buckle against the cracked window frame. He arched a skeptical brow at Patsy before continuing. *"—Cowboy Buddy?"*

"Uh." Patsy nervously touched the tip of her tongue to her lips. "Yes, Officer, that's true." What in heaven's name had they done now? Only seven years old, Marky and Mikey were basically good kids; they had simply lacked proper guidance at home.

"The Cowboy Buddy program here at the ranch allows children under twelve to accompany a teen in good standing—who would be the, uh, Cowboy Buddy—a mile into town for ice cream once a week," Patsy explained hurriedly, trying to curb her irritation with the twins.

Their parents had been killed making an illegal drug deal shortly after they were born, and since then, their harried young aunt had worked two jobs just to keep food on the table. During the unsupervised periods, the boys had become latchkey kids, falling through the cracks and fending for themselves the best they could. Already they were impressive pickpockets. The Artful Dodger had nothing on these two.

Marky and Mikey were Justin's pet project. He'd known their parents since childhood, and had promised their nineteen-year-old aunt he would look out for them until she got her life back together enough to come fetch them. So, she'd granted him temporary custody and headed off to parts unknown to take a breather and build a life for herself. He had a soft spot in his heart for the twins, and he was the closest thing to a father the boys had ever known. They worshiped him.

The officer wore a pained expression. "Then, perhaps you can tell me why I found them lifting candy down at Shen-Sheng's Oriental Food Market, over on Kim street. I didn't see a…ah, Cowboy Buddy anywhere in sight."

"Well, you see, Officer," Patsy attempted to explain as she narrowed her eyes at the two cherubic faces that smiled so innocently up at her, "unfortunately we are experiencing a shortage of Buddies this week, what with Thanksgiving vacation coming up and all…"

"Whatever." The officer waved an impatient hand. "Are you in charge here?" It was clear he had more important small fish to fry.

Patsy looked around the empty office. "Yes," she answered meekly, vowing to let Justin have it, next time she bumped into him.

"And that makes you responsible for these kids?"

She nodded. She guessed so. The Flannigan twins had frightened off or lost more than one well-meaning Cowboy Buddy in their time. Today's victim was probably no exception.

"So. If I leave them in your charge, you'll promise to keep them out of trouble?"

Gulping, Patsy nodded, wide-eyed. Well, she'd try anyway. She pursed her lips menacingly at the kids, hoping to scare them into submission.

They grinned devilishly up at her.

"Okay then," the overworked officer sighed and clapped a meaty hand around each scrawny arm as he remanded them to her care, "but I'm telling ya right now, if I so much as see one freckle where it shouldn't be, I'm haulin' 'em in. Got that?"

"Yes, sir!" Patsy threw her shoulders back and nodded crisply.

The boys grinned devilishly up at him.

Shaking his head, the officer left the trailer, muttering all the while about Cowboy Buddies and their obvious lack of responsibility.

Patsy turned her attention to her two charges. "Okay, boys. You're off the hook this time. Next time, I'm not going to cover for you. Do you understand?"

Shrugging, they smiled happily up at her, just before they started tearing around the office, giggling and chasing each other. Beyond the cracked window in the front door, Patsy could see the officer watching them for a moment from the interior of his squad car. With a shake of his head, he began to roll down the long, dusty driveway.

Grabbing each boy by the collar, Patsy pulled them up short. "Does Justin know what you've been up to?"

"No," Marky muttered.

"You're gonna tell?" Mikey wondered.

"Maybe." One brow arched thoughtfully. "Maybe not. But, before I make up my mind, Little Cowboys, I have a few chores for you to do so that you can earn some money to pay back the market for the candy you stole. So," she said, her voice no nonsense as she looked down at them, "here's the deal. You two mop the floor and wash out the sink in the back bathroom."

"Awww, geeeee," came the unified wail.

"Don't aw gee, me. You two owe me for bailing you out just now, and you owe me big. I'll figure out the rest of your duties later. But for now—" she handed Marky the mop and Mikey the pail "—get to work. It's late and I want my dinner." Turning, she shook her finger at them. "And for heaven's sake, don't steal anything!" Gesturing to the back of the trailer, she herded them to the bathroom.

* * *

"If you think we can afford it, let's go for it," Justin said over his shoulder as he ambled up the stairs and into the main office trailer. Buck was coming up the steps on his heels. "There aren't enough mounts to go around for the kids as it is. Sooner or later, we're going to have to break down and expand the herd."

"I hear ya," Buck grumbled, stomping his boots on the stoop then slamming the trailer door shut behind them. "Come on into my office. I've got some pretty decent leads on a few horses that would be just right for the intermediate class." Buck brushed passed Justin and pushed open the door to the tiny office he shared with Holly. "We can talk about 'em, but ultimately, the decision is yours."

"Okay," Justin murmured, his eyes scanning Patsy's desk as he moved by.

So. She'd gone home for the night. Why was he so disappointed? It wasn't as if he were on any kind of friendly, flirtatious, teasing-type terms with her. Even so, he felt like a little kid whose ribbon to his balloon had slipped off his wrist. The color in his day was floating out to join the setting sun.

He gave his head a sharp shake to clear it of this ridiculous train of thought. "Are you sure we can afford them? I mean, I'm willing to make do with the stock we have now."

Joining Buck in the cramped office, Justin flopped onto the couch and rested his aching dogs on the coffee table. He couldn't wait to get these boots off his feet and take a shower. His small quarters in the bunk trailer next door beckoned. His stomach was growling and he had half of a stale, cold pizza calling his name.

"Would you stop worrying?" Buck chuckled. "We can afford it. One way or another. Holly has Patsy working on a fund-raiser that should cover it."

Justin held up his hands. "Just asking." Ever since he'd

managed to graduate from college, he had been tucking away whatever extra money he didn't need for monthly bills for the house he'd been planning on building. Saving was simply part of his nature. Part of his means of survival. Since he and Darlene had split up last year he hadn't felt the immediate urge to break ground on the house, but lately his quarters were beginning to feel a little confining. And lonely.

That's probably why he liked hanging around the office whenever he wasn't working. There was always something going on. He really liked Holly and Buck, and then of course, these days, he could pick on Patsy.

So much for his social life.

It was all too true, he thought with a sigh. He'd spent so much time helping Holly and Buck get their project off the ground, he'd neglected his dating life. In a big way. Although, it was no surprise, really, that he hadn't rushed back into a relationship. He'd been burned. Darlene just never could seem to get over the idea that when it came to money—for now anyway—the ranch and his house plans came first.

Buck had offered to make him a partner in the Miracle House Ranch business and they were in the process of working out the logistics of such a partnership now. More than once Justin had tried to explain his reasons to Darlene, but she hadn't understood. She'd had an image to maintain and neither Justin's paycheck nor his apartment in the trailer had fit her bill.

Reaching up, he rubbed the muscles that pinched in his neck and shoulders. One of these days, he knew he was going to have to bite the bullet and throw himself into the dating scene again. But for now, anyway, he had more important things on his mind. Like horses. And blueprints for his house. And Marky and Mikey. And making sure those two kids felt loved and wanted.

Searching around in his drawer, Buck finally rooted out the list of horses for sale he was looking for and tossed it to Justin. "Take a look at these, and tell me what you think tomorrow."

"Okay," Justin mumbled, scanning the page.

Pushing himself from the desk, Buck stepped to his office door. "You want a sandwich, man? Holly's taking a nap up at the house, and I'm starving."

Justin thought about his refrigerator with the disintegrating pizza and grinned. "Yeah, that would be great. I could eat a horse." Reclining on the couch, he called, "No pun intended."

Buck's laughter rang out and Justin smiled to himself as he read up on available horseflesh. A few moments later, the phone rang and Buck, his arms filled with paper plates loaded with sandwiches and soda cans, nodded in the direction of the sound. "Get that for me, will ya, buddy?"

Dragging his feet off the coffee table, Justin reached over to Buck's desk and snatched the handset out of the cradle. "Yo?" he answered, accepting an overflowing paper plate from Buck as he spoke.

"Hello," a cool, feminine and decidedly sexy voice on the other end of the line purred. "Is Patsy Brubaker there?"

Cocking an interested brow, Justin glanced at the wall clock. After hours on a Saturday night. Was this one of Patsy's gal pals? She sounded like a bombshell. Shoot. Maybe he should begin thinking about kick-starting his social life a little sooner than planned. "Uh, Patsy? Brubaker?" he asked, stalling.

"Well, perhaps she doesn't go by her maiden name anymore?"

"Patsy? Our Patsy?" he wondered, catching Buck's eye and grinning.

"Who is it?" Buck asked.

Justin shrugged.

As the feminine voice continued to purr in his ear, the Flannigan twins came tearing down the hallway, a harried Patsy chasing them with a mop.

"Wait just a minute, you two," she barked, heading them off at the pass and pointing dramatically at the bathroom. "You're not done yet. Rinse and dry the floor."

"Awwww," the boys wailed, and slogged back to the sudsy linoleum.

"Hey, hang on," Justin instructed the caller. "You're in luck. She is here." He poked his head into the empty hallway. "At least she was a minute ago..."

"Oh, great," the cultured voice continued. "Do you suppose I could speak with her for a moment?"

"I'm sure that could be arranged," Justin said teasingly, not moving to summon Patsy. "But, are you sure you wouldn't rather just talk to me instead?"

Lilting laughter filtered into his ear. "Why, I'm sure we'll get an opportunity in the near future," she cooed breathily.

Returning like a damp prize fighter from the bathtub ring, Patsy entered her brother's office and found him scarfing the meager contents of the kitchenette as if he were on death row and this was his last supper.

"I heard the phone ring," she explained, flopping onto the couch next to Justin. Retraining her gaze, she watched as Justin chuckled cozily on the line to the mystery caller.

"Yeah, hold on, just a second." Holding the phone out to Patsy, he grinned engagingly. "It's for you."

With an exasperated sigh, Patsy wrested the phone from his hand, then turned her back on him. "Hello?" she barked impatiently into the phone. Lord only knew what Justin had been telling the caller.

"Hello," the sophisticated blast from the past answered. "I'll bet you don't know who this is."

"No?" The voice sounded vaguely familiar, and Patsy

searched her brain until it landed on the announcement for her ten-year class reunion.

Bitsy?

It was Bitsy! Wife of Bram, mother of Barron, Brianna and Bryce and real estate mogul extraordinaire. Her heart crowded into her throat and began to polka. Why on earth was Bitsy calling her? She'd thrown her bio away along with her harebrained plans to attend her reunion as this era's answer to John Glenn.

As calmly as she could, Patsy forced a smile into her voice. She would play it cool. If Bitsy discovered that she were nothing more than the receptionist and part-time dance instructor for the Miracle House Ranch, it would be all over the front pages of the *Willow Creek Gazette* by noon tomorrow. Hunching away from the two men who stared with such interest at the back of her head, Patsy lowered her voice, and cupped the mouthpiece with her palms.

The sultry voice continued. "It's Bitsy, from Willow Creek High? The private high school you attended ten years ago." Politely, Bitsy attempted to jog her memory.

"Umm..." Patsy pretended to think. "Bitsy?" she murmured into the mouthpiece.

She could feel Justin straining closer to better hear her conversation. She sighed.

"Oh. Yes. Bitsy. Hello there, uh, Bitsy. From Willow Creek High." There. Good. She was proud of the cool, rather aloof tone she'd managed to convey. Her mind raced frantically. Why ever would Bitsy be calling her? To inform her in person of the reunion? Oh dear. She needed a plausible excuse to get out of attending. *Surgery? Accident? Death in the family? Death of a co-worker?* she wondered grumpily, nudging Justin away from her shoulder.

"Get lost," she mouthed, and pushed against the firm wall of his chest with the palm of her hand. Gracious. The

flesh beneath his T-shirt was warm and rock hard beneath her fingertips. This served only to further fluster her.

Buck grinned and, ignoring his sandwich, leaned forward.

"It's so good to hear your voice, Patsy," Bitsy enthused. "Was that your husband who answered the phone? He sounds very sexy."

Caught completely off guard and not knowing what else to say, Patsy shrugged and glanced at Justin's handsome face, now fairly glowing with interest. She would answer the sexy part of the question.

"Uh, yes, he is…or sounds that way…yes."

"Well, anyway—" Bitsy's lilting laughter sparkled over the miles "—the reason I'm calling is to make sure that you're planning on attending our class reunion. I know you must be terribly busy with your fantastic life, but we were really hoping that you could come."

My fantastic life? What had Bitsy heard? With a slight frown, her gaze swept around the dusty, cramped quarters that made up Buck's office.

"You want to know if I'm attending the reunion?" Patsy gulped. What was her excuse again? "Uh…"

Buck and Justin grinned at each other and hovered even closer, trying to hear Bitsy on the other end of the line.

Stretching the phone cord to its limits, Patsy stood and moved to the doorway. She sent a murderous glance to the men. "I hadn't planned on it, Bitsy," she said, hedging. She still wasn't sure where this was going.

"Oh, *no!*" Bitsy sounded truly mortified.

"Oh, no?" Patsy chewed her lower lip and glanced at the guys. "Why oh, no?"

Standing, both Buck and Justin crowded at her side, straining to hear. Ignoring her frantic and angry hand gestures, they gleefully eavesdropped on her conversation.

"Do you remember Mrs. Renfru?" Bitsy queried breathlessly, her distress audible. "I know you're probably far too busy these days to sit around remembering any of us from Willow Creek High, but Mrs. Renfru was your dance teacher?''

"Yes…'' Patsy said, pushing her fingers to her lips, and shushing the guys. "I recall.''

She would never forget Mrs. Renfru. The darling, bright-eyed Mrs. Renfru was an old lady, even ten years ago. She'd been Patsy's favorite teacher, all through high school. Patsy had always gone above and beyond the call of duty on her dance recitals, in an effort to please the delightful, loving teacher. She would have done anything for her back then. Mrs. Renfru had instilled in Patsy her love for dance, and Patsy adored her to this day.

"Well,'' Bitsy continued, "anyway, this is Mrs. Renfru's last year of teaching. Did you know that?''

"No, no, I didn't. Please, give her my congratulations, Bitsy,'' Patsy said, trying to figure out a way to wrap up this miserable conversation. Justin's and Buck's sonorous breathing grew louder in her ear. Gracious. Bitsy must think she had some sort of debilitating lung problem.

"Oh, no!'' Bitsy cried. "I want you to do that yourself!''

Do what? "You do?'' Perplexed, Patsy frowned.

"Yes! You can congratulate her yourself at the big re-tirement party we are going to throw for her during one of the reunion functions! We figured that would be a great time to do it because a lot of her old students will be in town for the holidays. Anyway,'' Bitsy chattered on, build-ing up momentum and volume and enthusiasm, just like the good old days on the cheer squad, "when I told her that you had at one time danced with a famous Irish dance troop in Europe…''

Justin and Buck snorted.

"Patsy? Are you still there?''

"Uh, yes,'' Patsy grunted, whirling around and shoving the two men out of the office and slamming the door in their curious faces as hard as she could and still sound the cool sophisticate. "Just the kids."

"Oh, I know all about that," Bitsy sympathized. "Okay, where was I? Oh, yes. The dance. When we told Mrs. Renfru about your fantastic dance experiences in Europe, well, my heavens, she said that she couldn't believe it, and that you were the crown jewel in her career as a dance teacher."

"The crown jewel in her career? Me?" Patsy asked dully.

Justin and Buck guffawed rudely from the other side of the door. The pitter-pat of little feet thundered down the hallway, as Marky and Mikey, having deemed the bathroom ready for inspection, arrived to add to Patsy's sudden migraine.

"Oh, yes!" Bitsy continued. "Why, Mrs. Renfru nearly broke down and cried with joy when she heard the news. She insists that you come and bring your lovely, talented and gifted family."

"My…family?" Patsy held the receiver away from her head and stared at it in horror. What the devil? This was like something straight out of the scene in Mary Poppins where the ad the children had written for a nanny had floated up the chimney and magically made it to Mary. How had the bio that she thought she'd thrown away ended up in Bitsy's hands? She *had* thrown it away…hadn't she? She racked her brain to remember. So much paperwork came and went on any given day. Could she have mailed it?

"Definitely. Goodness, everyone always knew you were most likely to succeed, but we never dreamed your success would be so, so…faboo! Marriage to a prominent surgeon, two gifted children, a stunning career… My stars! How do you do it?" Bitsy gushed.

Face flaming with mortification, Patsy began to feel faint and she couldn't be sure, but it seemed to her that the room had begun to spin. Somehow, her bio had been mailed. Pregnant Gayle helped her out on some days. Would she have mailed it by mistake? Obviously she had. Sinking to the couch, Patsy stared at the wall.

"Patsy?" Bitsy chirped. "Can you and your husband make it?"

The weight of the two men, coupled with the added stress of the two boys, was more than the old door frame could handle, and with a pop, all four Curious Georges suddenly found themselves standing in the office.

"You want my...husband to come, too?"

Justin rolled his eyes at Buck, and planting his hands on his hips swung his mischievous gaze to Patsy. "Oh, honey," he called, a wide grin splitting his handsome face, "are you going to be on the phone all night? I need to call the hospital, I have a face-lift in an hour."

Squeezing his eyes tightly shut, Buck clutched the broken door frame and bit back the laughter.

"Yes," Bitsy urged, "you must bring your husband. He sounds simply divine."

Unable to help himself, Justin continued to harass her. "Sweetheart," he called, "do you want to drop the kids off at college in the morning, or shall I?"

Buck, a nearly painful expression crossing his face, pushed the kids out of the way and darted into the hallway. His laughter exploded from the kitchenette.

Patsy glared after him, then turned the poisonous darts in her eyes to Justin.

"Is that the reunion committee, honey?" Justin continued, shouting down the hall for Buck's benefit. "Tell them we'll be happy to attend! I'll just shuffle a few nose jobs, and you can skip the next dance tour..."

Howling, Buck tumbled out the front door of the office trailer, and fell to the ground laughing. The kids, unsure of exactly what was so funny, but loving the hilarity, ran after him. Justin moved back into the office and took Buck's chair behind the desk. He watched Patsy with an arched brow, a smug smile tugging at the corners of his mouth.

In order to block out his probing stare, Patsy closed her eyes, took a deep calming breath and pushed the phone back up to her ear just in time to catch the end of Bitsy's perky diatribe. No wonder she was in the million dollar club as a Realtor, Patsy thought dizzily. Bitsy droned on and on until Patsy feared she might spontaneously combust from sheer panic.

From the sound of things, they were planning an entire weekend around her darned phony bio. They wanted her to dance at the gala event, Saturday night of the reunion. The *Gala!* Oh, good grief! It was a *joke,* for crying out loud! She glanced at Justin, his arms folded imposingly across his broad chest, his brow knitted accusingly. Didn't anyone get it? *It was a practical joke!* Was she the only one who could see that?

"Uh, Bitsy." Patsy managed to interrupt for a second. Dropping her elbows to her knees, she rubbed her forehead and wondered how to break the news to Bitsy. It was time to tell the truth, she sighed, squirming under Justin's judicial stare.

Unfortunately Bitsy had no intention of letting her get a word in edgewise. "And, of course, Mrs. Renfru is inviting her whole family—grandchildren and all—to the retirement party to watch you present her service award. It would be so nice if you could do this, considering everything that's happened since her terrible accident. It's so sad."

Patsy froze. *Accident?* What accident?

"Anyway, to hear her talk—luckily she can still talk— why, you would think you were some kind of movie star!"

She nattered on for a while longer about her wonderful plans, while Patsy sat rigid with shock. Before she knew it, Patsy heard herself agreeing to go to the reunion, to dance at the big party, to talk to the press and to present the award. Anything to get the rabid Bitsy off the line.

Perhaps she could catch the chicken pox between now and then, she thought hopefully.

After Bitsy finally rang off, claiming that she would be in touch to keep her abreast of all the latest plans, Patsy, still shell-shocked, hung up and sat frozen to her seat.

"So," Justin sighed, disappointment tingeing his words. He pointed at her with one of Buck's pencils. "You decided to cop out and send in that stupid bio anyway."

"No," she whispered dazedly. "I didn't."

"You didn't?" Justin was puzzled.

"No. I didn't."

"You didn't." Justin was skeptical.

"No. Really. I didn't! I have no idea how she got a hold of it."

Justin snorted.

"No! Honest," Patsy cried, suddenly coming to life. Suddenly realizing what had just happened. "I thought I threw it away. It must have gotten mixed up with the outgoing mail somehow."

Slowly Justin shook his head and stroked his five o'clock shadow with his thumb. "So why didn't you tell her that?"

"I couldn't get a word in sideways with a crowbar!" she cried, hating his arrogant, holier-than-thou attitude. "You were here! You saw how she blathered on."

"You could have interrupted and told her the truth." His lazy gaze flitted over her, his eyes at half-mast.

"She caught me off guard, okay?" Patsy shouted, leaning forward, her eyes sparking with fury. "Next time, *honey*, I'll hand *you* the phone and let you explain our family situation in person!"

Justin had the good grace to blush. "Okay, I admit..."

"That's right! You were certainly no help in leading poor Bitsy to the real story, *darling*," she continued, not bothering to let him finish his sentence. "If you are so hell-bent on telling her the blasted truth, then pick up the phone and *tell her yourself!*" Patsy spat, gearing up for a fight she'd wanted to pick with him since her second day on the job. "You'll find her phone number in the Rolodex on my desk!"

"I..."

"And another thing! You are so smug, Mr. Truth, Justice and the American Way! You never make mistakes, do you? You never care what people think of you, do you?" Fired up, she moved across the office to stand in front of Buck's desk. With furious fingers, she stabbed at his blotter, her eyes locking with Justin's. "Ohhh no! You just sit in judgment of other people. People you don't know anything about."

"Wait just a min..."

Blue sparks of rage darted from her eyes to his dark green ones. He was going to listen, and he was going to listen good. She was sick to death of his condescending attitude. How dare he? Who the hell did he think he was?

Tossing her mop of disheveled hair over her shoulder, Patsy continued. "You don't know me! You don't know anything about me. Yet you have judged me and closed your mind, and treated me like something you stepped in out in the paddock since day one. You think I'm some spoiled little rich girl. You think I was just hired for this job because my brother felt sorry for me, floating my life away in the pool. You think Buck and Holly thought I needed a project. Something to get me out of the mansion for a little while. That's just what you think!" she cried, leaning across the desk and really getting into his face.

"I can tell by the look in your eyes. You think I'm taking a job away from some poor person who needs work. Well, I have news for you, *buddy,*" she informed him, her arms spread on the desk, supporting her now as she released her turmoil.

"I—"

Patsy cut him off as he tried to interject, sure that she sounded like a she-devil, but was beyond caring.

"*I* am a poor person who needs work! I can type at the speed of light, answer the phone with zest in the fiery bowels of an unair-conditioned furnace, and file like a maniac."

A small smile tipped Justin's mouth, but quickly disappeared.

"As of two months ago, I am no longer my daddy's little princess. I'm dirt poor and living in a shack that makes your apartment look like…like…the *Ritz!* I ride my bike to work. Not for the exercise, but because my car—and I use that term loosely—ran out of gas and I can't afford to fill the stupid tank!" She gestured wildly to her dance togs. "Do you think I enjoy wearing these to work, day in and day out?"

Justin frowned. "I…"

"Well, I don't! But I'm too proud to go crawling back to my father for a handout. I have a closet stuffed with designer clothes at his house, but you know what? I don't want them anymore.

"I'll be damned if I can't make it on my own in this world. I'm—" tears pooled unnoticed in her eyes "—not Big Daddy Brubaker's daughter for nothing! And you, Mr. High and Mighty, you're not the only one who can… can—" she sniffed and swiped in irritation at the tears that streamed down her cheeks "—thrive in the face of—" she took a deep breath *"—adversity!"*

Having finished her diatribe and run out of wind, Patsy sagged.

"Patsy, I…"

"Save it," she snapped with a ragged sigh and, mustering her last shred of dignity, pushed off the desk. Moving toward the door, she paused in the broken frame. "I'm going to go get on my bike now, and ride home and try to figure out how I'm going to let poor little old Mrs. Renfru down. Then, I'm going to call Bitsy and apologize for the mistake. Sooner or later, they are going to realize that I am the one *least* likely to succeed anyway. It might as well be tonight."

And with that, Patsy shuffled out of the office, leaving Justin staring after her with an open mouth.

Chapter Four

From the address Buck had given him, Justin assumed that this must be the place. Although, as he parked his motorcycle in the building's lot and unbuttoned the last button of his shirt against the sluggish evening air, he could scarcely believe that Patsy Brubaker would ever set foot on this side of town, let alone live here.

After having digested Patsy's rampage, Justin knew he needed to set the record straight between them or working together in the future would be impossible. Might as well do it tonight. Besides, as much as he hated to admit it, she had a point or two. He'd misjudged her. He hadn't been as friendly to her as he might have been to someone who didn't remind him quite so much of Darlene. He owed her an apology.

So, he'd wormed her address out of Buck, jumped on his motorcycle and set out through the long shadows of the setting sun to find Patsy's place.

However never, in his wildest dreams, had he expected Patsy's place to be in this firetrap of a building, perched

on the edge of town near the railroad tracks. Hell, he'd
spent more than a few of his formative years in an inner-
city slum that was better off than this dump.

Raggedy laundry billowed in the hot breezes and was
strung higgledy-piggledy from lopsided balcony to balcony.
On the ground, a group of filthy kids played King of the
Hill on an old junk mattress, happily jumping on the rusty
and broken springs as if this constituted their complex's
playground. Music vibrated from one apartment, the bass
guitars registering at least a two on the Richter scale. The
smells of something fried, something burned and something
rotten wafted in the air, and at the far end of the building,
a dog barked nonstop.

Approaching the complex, Justin gripped the rickety iron
railing and took the stairs two at a time, his shirttails flapping behind him. Once he was on the second floor, he began searching for apartment 2A. Several rather seedy-
looking characters lurked in a doorway marked 2B.

As Justin passed, the hairs on the back of his neck began
to tingle. These boys were watching him, sizing him up.
His days on the streets gave him a sixth sense about what
they were thinking. Fists tightening convulsively, he strode
purposefully past, not looking in their direction. This was
no place for a beautiful woman like Patsy to live, he
thought, a muscle jumping in his jaw. This was no place
for a not so beautiful woman to live. Hot damn, this was
no place for a gorilla to live. Buck would go ballistic, if
he knew his baby sister lived in a hellhole like this.

There was a rustling sound behind him, as he made his
way beyond the group, and he tensed. He knew their kind.
He'd been one. A street tough. Knowing his adversary, he
mentally prepared himself for a fight.

He stopped midstride.

Shoulders square, eyes narrow, he slowly turned around
and met the eyes of Patsy's scumball neighbors. After a

brief stare down, the scumballs disappeared back into 2B behind a cloud of cigarette smoke. Justin blew out a breath of relief and ran his hands through his hair. No way was Patsy going to stay in this godforsaken building. Not if he had anything to say about it.

He knocked, then waited at the door of 2A.

"Who is it?" a tiny, fearful voice demanded.

"Patsy?" Justin wondered if he had the right address after all.

"Who wants to know?" hissed the suspicious voice.

"It's me. Justin. Justin Lassiter."

"Justin!" Patsy squealed and, fumbling with several locks, finally had the door opened wide enough for her to reach out, grip his shirt and yank him inside. As she realized what she had done, her tremulous smile of relief was replaced by one of cool sophistication.

"What are you doing here?" Her eyes flicked curiously to his open shirt.

Before answering, Justin turned around, secured the door with the half dozen locks he found there, then barged past her to secure the rest of the doors and windows.

"What are you doing?" Patsy moaned. "It's already too muggy to breathe."

"Are you trying to get yourself killed?" Justin asked, propping a wooden chair under the knob of her door.

"No," she crabbed, running over to a window he'd just locked and throwing it open again. "Quite the opposite. I'm trying not to suffocate."

"Okay," Justin conceded with a grin. "One window. That's all."

He moved her fan in front of the window, to draw the cooler air. Coming back into her living room, he stared at her. She was wearing cutoff sweatpants, a ratty old T-shirt with the neck and arms torn off and her feet were bare except for the dabs of pink on her toenails. Her thick, sun-streaked curls were swept up into a ponytail at the top of her head and to Justin she looked like a schoolgirl. She was also just about the cutest thing he'd ever laid eyes on.

Swallowing, he attempted to lasso his runaway pulse.

Patsy sighed. "Justin…what are you doing here?"

Crossing his arms over his chest, he leaned against the wall and arched a curious brow.

"That's a very good question. One that I might ask of you. Why don't you invite me in to sit down? We'll discuss it. And this time, if you don't mind—" he felt a smile tugging at the corner of his mouth "—I'd like to get a word in here and there."

Her cheeks grew pink at his light admonition and casting her eyes to the floor, Patsy gestured to her "living room" area.

"Sorry, I only have the one chair," she explained, gesturing at the dilapidated love seat. "It came with the apartment. I pay $1.50 more in rent for it each month, and $2.00 extra for the futon mattress in the bedroom."

They should be paying her to store the hideous thing here, Justin thought, his lips forming a grim line as he gingerly lowered his body onto the lumpy little couch.

"Can I get you something to drink?" Patsy wondered as she moved the few feet that took her over to the loudly churning refrigerator.

"Ice water would be fine."

"Good," she giggled, "because that's all I have. That, and a bowl of chipped ice to snack on. I'll go grocery shopping tomorrow. I didn't have time today."

Loud, argumentative voices filtered through the wall that divided apartment 2A from 2B. The hostility that was brewing next door was nearly palpable in its intensity. Ignoring the curses that could have peeled the remaining paint off the kitchen walls, Patsy continued to prepare their drinks, seemingly oblivious to the danger that lurked just beyond the wall.

It was all Justin could do not to grab her and hightail it back to his place where he could keep an eye on her. Obviously she had no idea that living here was inviting disaster. This was not her father's mansion. There were no guards and security systems here. No gun-toting father or brothers to protect her. Uncomfortable in the lumpy love seat, Justin fidgeted, and wondered how to best convince her that she needed to move. Immediately if not sooner.

Returning to the living room, Patsy set two glasses of water on the makeshift coffee table along with the bowl of ice. Looking around, she pondered the question of where to sit, a delicate forefinger hovering at her full lips. Before he'd had time to think twice, Justin heard himself inviting her to join him on the love seat, where he could protect her, if need be.

"Sit down," he commanded, patting the lumpy cushion at his side.

Hesitating for a moment, Patsy shrugged. It wasn't as if she had any other choice.

"Okay." Once she settled into the far side of her seat, up against the arm of the chair, she shot him a quick smile. "So," she said and expelled a long breath, "here we are."

"Why?"

"Why?" Patsy frowned. "You're the one who came to see me, remember?"

"I know. Why *here?* In case you haven't noticed, this isn't exactly Mr. Rogers's neighborhood."

Curses exploded next door, and Patsy's apartment shook as either a piece of furniture or a body—Justin couldn't be sure which—was slammed against the connecting wall.

Patsy clicked her tongue and squinted at him. "Like I told you earlier," she said and lifted her hands in a resigned manner, "it's all I can afford."

The tinkling sound of glass shattering filtered through her open window.

"Why don't you just take a loan from your dad?" Justin wondered, glancing around and searching for the most expedient emergency exits. "Something that would get you settled in a little...*safer* area of town."

"Like I told you earlier," Patsy reiterated a little more slowly, bristling as she pursed her lips at him. "I can take care of myself. I don't take handouts from anyone, let alone Big Daddy. Especially not Big Daddy."

"Not even when your safety depends on it?"

"It's safe enough here."

More heated cursing exploded from next door, followed by an eerie silence.

Justin snorted. "Yeah, right."

"Hey, I look both ways before I go out my front door," she countered defensively.

"And then what do you do? Shout for the landlord to cover you as you ride down the street? Surely you are aware that the boys who live next door are not members of the local church choir."

"They're okay." Nervously she twisted her fingers together as they lay in her lap.

"C'mon, Patsy, tell the truth. They're thugs, and you know it."

"So what?" As if to stop wringing her hands, she looped her arms around her smooth, tan legs. "I don't bother them, they don't bother me."

Justin felt his mouth drop at her attitude. Wasn't she even a little bit afraid? Most women would thank their lucky stars for a white knight like him to come riding to their rescue. But, Patsy wasn't most women. She was as stubborn as a window long painted shut and twice as hard to move.

"Okay, they haven't bothered you. Not yet, anyway. Listen, Patsy, they could kill you without even intending to!'' he exclaimed. "I think you should move. As soon as possible. Tonight. Right now.'' He inclined his head toward the front door. "Let's go.'' Buck would thank him for this in the morning. He simply could not, in good conscience, let the boss's sister stay here another day. It wasn't ethical.

Patsy laughed incredulously. "I'm not going anywhere. Besides, who asked you to come barging over here to tell me how to live? Or where to live for that matter?''

"No one. But your brother will blow a gasket as soon as he gets a load of this place.''

She stopped laughing and narrowed her snapping blue gaze at him. "You will leave Buck out of this, please.''

Arching an "excuse me" brow, Justin looked and tried to find the spot where the marbles were leaking from her head. "Ahh…no. I don't *think* so. Not when there is a perfectly good apartment sitting empty in the trailer next to mine on the ranch.''

"Oh, forget that!'' Patsy's ponytail swayed vehemently as she shook her head. "I'm not moving to the ranch.''

"Why not? You wouldn't have to commute, you could even get rid of that gas-guzzling car you never seem to drive, if you wanted to.''

She gasped. "Oh, no. I'm not selling my car.''

"How come?''

"Because it cost me *two hundred dollars!*'' Wide-eyed, Patsy looked at him with barely disguised shock. "That's a lot of money, bucko.''

Justin rolled his eyes. "Okay. I get it. You like your car, you like your apartment, you like your independence and you want me to mind my own business.'' A grudging grin of admiration tinged the corners of his mouth. She had spunk. He had to give her that.

Something thudded repeatedly against the wall from next

door, then sounded as if it was being dragged across the floor.

Justin sighed. Either spunk or insanity. He hadn't figured out which yet.

"Very good." Patsy's responding smile was impish. "So. What are you doing here, besides trying to 'dis' my nifty digs?"

"You've lived next door to a gang too long, I can see that already," he groaned. "Well," he said, settling back in his seat with his ice water and crossing his ankle over his knee, "the real reason I stopped by was to apologize."

"Apologize?" Patsy echoed. "For what, exactly?"

"For the way I've been treating you, since you came to work at the ranch. You were right. I had preconceived ideas of you."

"That's okay," Patsy murmured, lifting her brows and letting them fall. "You weren't so far wrong."

Justin's eyes traveled slowly around her bare little apartment. The only "luxury" he could see was a phone. "No. I was. Really." The hounds of hell couldn't have encouraged Darlene into this apartment. She'd have sooner died.

"Well, in any event, you'll be happy to know that I called Bitsy Hart when I got home." Shifting in her seat, Patsy brought her leg up under her knee, and leaned slightly toward him.

"What'd she say?"

"Nothing yet. She wasn't home. I left my number, and asked her to call me as soon as possible." Pushing some unruly strands of flyaway silk away from her face, she brought her eyes to Justin's.

"That's great. You must have figured out what you are going to say to her." Justin held her gaze, and resisted the impulse to reach out and touch her hand. Her arm. The high bones of her sculptured cheek. There was something so…compelling about her. Then again, Darlene could be compelling on occasion. Thrusting his hands beneath his thighs, Justin leaned back in order to create a little distance between them.

"Yep. I'm simply going to tell the truth."

Justin nodded as a bud of pride bloomed in his chest for her. "That's probably for the best."

Patsy sighed. "I know you're right. It's just that I really hate to let Mrs. Renfru down."

"Mrs. Renfru?" Justin didn't follow.

"My dance teacher. They want me to present her with an award of some sort. She's retiring this year. She's also the reason I fell in love with dance."

Reaching up, Justin stroked the stubble on his chin with his knuckles. "I had one of those once."

"A dance teacher?"

He chuckled. "No. A mentor. Someone who taught me about passion."

Patsy wrinkled her nose warily. "Do I really want to hear this?"

"A passion for ranching, you goof."

"Ah. Now *that* I understand, having grown up on a ranch."

She smiled up at him, and Justin felt the wall he'd spent the last two months erecting between them begin to crumble. She was beguiling. He'd have to watch himself around her. It wouldn't do to go and get all hung up on the sister of his future partner. Besides, this leopard simply had different spots. She was still a Darlene.

In spite of his trepidation when it came to getting to know Patsy Brubaker, he found himself suddenly opening up to her in a way he hadn't opened up to anyone for a long time. For the next thirty golden minutes—in the surprising silence that hailed from next door—Justin and Patsy entertained each other with stories of their youth and of the significant people that had made a real difference in their lives. And, though her background was different, Patsy nodded and murmured, letting him know that she could relate to him on many different levels.

Feeling completely relaxed now in each other's company, Justin had sprawled out on his end of the love seat. His feet were propped on the coffee table that Patsy had fashioned from two suitcases seated on a stack of bricks. Eyes at half-mast, he regarded her lazily as she spoke of her childhood in a house full of male ranchers, made special because of a dance teacher who cared.

He wondered what it would feel like to be the object of such total devotion. Mesmerized by the animation in her face as she waxed poetic about Mrs. Renfru, Justin studied Buck Brubaker's younger sister, and learned. She had the classic Brubaker dimples that appeared and disappeared as she smiled and laughed. Her eyes were the bluest shade of cornflower blue, fringed with heavy, dark lashes that needed no makeup, and her teeth, perfectly straight and pearly white, sparkled as she spoke. Like some kind of poster child for perfection, he thought, awestruck by her physical beauty. Even her hair, thick and curly, sun-kissed and streaked with gossamer lights, was something out of a shampoo commercial.

But he was beginning to realize, though he hated to admit it, even to himself, that there was more to Patsy Brubaker than met the eye. Much more. Perhaps he'd misread her. She really seemed to understand what he'd been through as a boy. And he didn't feel as if she judged him. Not the way Darlene had, at any rate. Maybe Buck's younger sister wasn't all bad after all.

Lulling him, her sultry voice, softened by a slight Southern accent, filled his head, mellowing him and giving him a taste of what it had been like to be a child in the Brubaker household.

"...and so that's why it's going to be so difficult to tell

Bitsy the truth. And it will be even harder because Bitsy said that Mrs. Renfru had been in some kind of accident.''

Justin roused himself from his reverie enough to respond. "She has?"

Patsy's ponytail bobbed emphatically. "Yes. She didn't say what kind of accident, actually, but from the way she spoke about Mrs. Renfru being lucky to still talk, I have a feeling it was bad."

"I'm sorry." Genuine sympathy crowded into his throat.

"Me, too."

Justin smiled ruefully. "About everything."

Patsy reached out and lightly patted his knee. "Don't worry. I know I have been known to come off like a spoiled deb on occasion."

His smile blossomed into a grin. "Well, at any rate, I shouldn't have given you such a hard time about the things you were writing on your reunion form. It was none of my business."

Lightly bunching her shoulders, Patsy sighed. "No...I know I shouldn't have even written those crazy things down on my biography. Even in jest. It's just that when I see that everyone else is so successful, and I'm having such a...a...hard time...you know...getting started..." Exhaling heavily, she looked around the sorry little apartment she now called home. "And now...now they're all going to know I'm a failure. Oh well."

"You're not a failure."

"I suppose that's a matter of opinion." A tiny smile touched her lips and was gone. "Can you believe that I told them I was married to a guy named Dr. Oscar Madison?"

Incredulous laughter swirled in his belly and bubbled into his throat. *"Oscar Madison?"* Justin pinched the bridge of his nose with his thumb and forefinger and squeezed his eyes tightly shut. "Wasn't he one of the guys on the 'Odd Couple'?"

"Yes. The messy one." She chuckled and drank the last of her water. "I don't know why he popped into my mind, exactly, except that I must have been thinking about the mess on my desk." She held up her water glass. "I need a refill. Can I get you one?"

"Sure."

"Sorry I don't have anything more fancy to offer you."

"Water's fine."

Pulling herself to her feet, she walked to the kitchen and filled the bowl with ice again, then filled the two glasses with water. "I don't have any munchies, either. I've been snacking on ice chips the past couple of days to try to stay cool…" she explained, gathering all the containers into her arms and heading back to the living room.

The phone rang before she made it to the coffee table.

"Ohh, I'll bet that's Bitsy," she nervously predicted. Backing up to the wall phone between the living room and kitchen areas, she gripped the bowl the best she could and reached for the phone. Ice slid out of the bowl and bounced around on the thirty-year-old green shag carpeting.

Justin stood to offer assistance.

"I'm fine," she murmured.

She tilted her head low in order to bring the phone to her mouth. "Hello?"

Bitsy's voice droned into the room. "Patsy? It's me, Bitsy? From Willow Creek High?"

"Yes, Bitsy," Patsy chirped as she slowly backed toward the kitchen and tried to balance the slippery bowl and two glasses. The phone cord, stretching tightly, tugged on her arms as she moved. "Thank you, uh, so much for, uh, returning my call. Listen, Bitsy," she began, bringing her knee up to keep the glass from slipping out from under her arm. "Uh, I, uh, wanted to tell you that I'm so sorry about my reunion biography." She inched toward the counter, hop skipping as she used her knee for support. "It was all a big...oops...uh, oh...darn!"

The bowl—having finally escaped the confines of her arms—leapt to freedom, where it crashed and broke into a thousand pieces on the kitchen floor. The glasses were in hot pursuit.

A cacophony of pithy epitaphs thundered through the walls from 2B. The sound of running footsteps vibrated the floorboards, as shouting ensued. Justin tensed for battle. Patsy seemed more concerned with the mess on the floor.

"Doggone it," she huffed, staring in dismay at the broken glass, then turning her baleful gaze to Justin. "And those were most of my dishes," she lamented.

"Patsy? Are you still there?" Bitsy's concerned voice buzzed across the line and into the room. "Patsy, is everything all right?"

Justin reached for the phone. "I'll talk to her while you go get a pair of shoes and the vacuum." He hoped his expression brooked no argument. As soon as Bitsy hung up, they were getting the hell out of here. She would need shoes for that.

"I don't have a vacuum."

"Then get a broom, or some newspaper, or something," Justin urged. "Before you cut yourself. And put some shoes on. I'll keep her company."

Patsy grinned. "That's right," she whispered, "I forgot that you and Bitsy are old phone pals." Laughing, she scuttled out of the room to find a pair of sneakers and a dustpan.

"Hello?" Bitsy squawked. "Is anyone there?"

"Bitsy?" Justin tucked the phone between his ear and shoulder and backed toward 2B to keep tabs on the violence. A fight had broken out and was reaching full swing. The sounds of fists connecting with faces and the foul language that accompanied was so loud, Justin could barely hear what Bitsy was saying. He needed to get this gal off the line so that he could call 911.

"Uh, Bitsy? I'm sorry, you'll have to speak up. The uh, uh…" Quickly he tried to think of a way to explain the battle that was taking place next door without taking all night. "The…I'm sorry, about the noise here, it's just that we were sitting down to…to…our dinner and…Patsy's having trouble with the…the oven…"

More glass shattered next door, followed by a stream of hair-curling language, the likes of which Justin hadn't heard in years. The walls in this place were paper thin.

"Sounds like she could use a hand," Bitsy intoned dryly.

"Uh, yes," he said, "well, anyway, she's a little busy with the roast, so she asked me to keep you company for a min…"

What sounded like gunshots rang out. Instinctively Justin dove behind the minuscule sofa for cover.

Oblivious, Bitsy continued. "Oh, that's okay. You must be Patsy's husband. I *never* forget a voice! Dr. Madison, right?"

Justin rolled his eyes and sat up, pulling the phone cord from where it was tangled around his feet. "Uh, yeah, right, she did say Dr. Madison. Well, uh, listen, Bitsy, that's what she put down on the form, but I…"

"I know. I thought, what a coincidence. He has the same name as that guy on the 'Odd Couple,'" Bitsy enthused. "I'll bet you take a lot of ribbing about that. You know, I have an Uncle named, get ready, *Michael Douglas!* Can you believe that? What are the odds?"

"I…I…would imagine…pretty good, actually…" What the hell was he doing having a conversation about celebrities and their namesakes at this time for? Justin gripped the phone between his ear and shoulder and, crawling on his hands and knees, he moved from behind the love seat to the front window and peered into the darkness. Shadowy figures, shouting and cursing as they went, ran across the parking lot headed straight for—and Justin could only guess here—apartment 2B. He glanced around for a weapon that he could use when the time came. And it was coming. Soon.

Bitsy was still blathering. "Well, we still tease him about that. Anyway, I can tell you all about it in person at the reunion. I'm just needing to talk to Patsy for a minute and make sure she's still dancing."

"*Ahhh,* yes, well," Justin tried to explain, "could Patsy call you back? She needs to talk to you about the dancing and all..."

"Oh, I can hang on. I really need to firm up the fact that she will be here to entertain the troops, as soon as possible. I know that she will be a wonderful asset to our party!" Her breathy enthusiasm gushed across the lines.

"Well, that's what I'm trying to tell you," he hissed, as he grabbed Patsy's umbrella from behind the soiled yellow draperies that hung limply at the living-room window. The shouting between the faction in the parking lot and the faction in the apartment escalated. "Bitsy," he grunted, yanking on the phone cord as he duck-walked to the front door. "Listen, I have to get off the line now. We've got kind of an emergency here."

"Of course. I know how it is for doctors," Bitsy chirped. "Could you just tell me if Patsy will be dancing for sure?"

How could he tell her that? Patsy wanted to be the one to explain the situation. It wasn't his place. "You need to talk to Patsy," he whispered. "In fact, the reason she called in the first place is that she wanted to let you know that the information on her biography is all wrong. I can't go into the details at the moment..."

"Wrong? Well now, to tell you the truth it was kind of hard to read in spots. But you tell her not to worry. We got it all figured out. Mrs. Renfru is thrilled that she's going to come down and bring you and the kids."

"The kids?" Justin mumbled, peering out the peephole. The unseemly crowd in the parking lot was growing. He *really* needed to call 911.

"Your two talented and gifted children?"

"Oh, yes, right. She told me about that…listen, Bitsy…"

"Then we can expect the whole family? Great! Mrs. Renfru will be delighted. You know, when she heard that Patsy was going to dance for her, well, the tears in her eyes…" Bitsy sighed heavily. "It was just so…sweet."

"Sweet, mmm-hmm, yeah." Justin bit out his reply impatiently.

"Okay. Tell Patsy that she's getting us out of a terrible jam. Our last entertainment idea canceled, so we were counting on her. What a relief. We'll print the final press releases tonight and send them out on the Internet. Tell her we're counting on her. I don't think I could bear another cancellation."

The thunder of machine-gun spray reverberated throughout the parking lot, followed by screams of terror.

"Tell Patsy to be careful with that roast," Bisty advised, concerned. "We don't want to lose our only entertainment."

Justin grunted as he rolled across the floor to the relative safety of the love seat. "Listen, Bitsy, I gotta go."

"That's fine. I must dash off myself. Drinks are being served. I have the reunion committee meeting over at my place tonight, for a planning party. So, Dr. Madison, I'll put you and Patsy and the kids down for Friday, Saturday and Sunday. That's just what I needed to know to finalize our plans tonight and get the wheels put into motion! Thanks for the info, I'll fax the newspaper immediately about Patsy's performance. Bye-bye now!"

And with that cheerful sign-off, she was gone. Letting

go of the phone, it flew out of his hand and ricocheted across the room and crashed into the wall that divided 2A from 2B. The sharp crack was the only impetus needed to begin an all-out war between the parking lot and the folks next door.

A moment later, unable to locate the dustpan, Patsy trotted back into the living room, only to find herself grabbed from behind and thrown to the floor. A rough hand covered her mouth, preventing the scream that welled in her throat from coming to the surface.

Chapter Five

Chapter Five

Patsy emerged from Justin's bathroom, feeling conspicuous dressed in nothing but one of his work shirts. Tugging on the tails, she did her best to disguise her thighs, but the sides between the tails were short. Awkwardly she skipped into his living room and hopped onto his couch where she covered her lap with a pillow.

While Justin puttered in the kitchen, Patsy's eyes traveled slowly around the single-wide trailer that he called home. It was cozy in spite of the fact that it was an exact duplicate of the office trailer where she worked, next door. There were bookcases stuffed with classics, and his stereo speakers alone must have cost him more than the trailer was worth. Strains of something light and jazzy played in the background. The furniture was leathery and manly, and there was a pile of colorful afghans that Patsy was sure some motherly type had made just for him. Framed photographs of friends lined the walls, and a few healthy plants gave the room a homey touch. In fact, for some strange reason, Patsy felt more at home here in this apartment of

Justin's than she ever had in her bedroom suite at her father's house.

Curious.

Humming a tuneless song under his breath, Justin busied himself in the kitchen and Patsy tried to remember the last time she'd eaten. Breakfast? Stomach growling, she wondered what that fabulous smell was wafting so temptingly through the air. She couldn't be sure, but she was willing to hazard a guess that it was Salisbury steak. Was he a gourmet cook as well as a superhero? Something tugged at her heartstrings, rearranging the opinions she'd originally formed of Justin. Perhaps he wasn't as bad as she had believed for these many weeks of working together at the ranch. After all, any man who could produce the fantastic aromas that emanated from the kitchen couldn't be all that bad.

Moving up on her knees, she strained to see him as he worked in the kitchen. *Good heavens above.* Did the man have any idea how handsome he was?

There was a masculine air about him that was undeniable. The slight swagger as he worked spoke of his carefree attitude and self-confidence, and the twinkle in his eyes revealed that he could laugh at himself. A permanent half smile was chiseled into the corner of his mouth giving him an almost haughty air that—as Patsy was discovering—was misleading. And the tiny dent in his chin gave him an arrogant look that she'd resented on more than one occasion. Tonight, however, she was finding him quite agreeable, both to look at, and to be rescued by.

Seeming to feel her gaze, Justin glanced up and caught her peering over the back of his couch.

Busted. Darn. Feeling the heat radiating up her neck, Patsy sank back into her seat and pulled one of the more colorful afghans over her bare legs.

Crinkles of amusement forked at the corners of Justin's

eyes as he stood in his kitchen waiting for the microwave to finish their dinner.

"That shirt has never looked so good," he commented as the timer began to buzz.

Patsy ducked her head and fiddled with the frayed cording around the edge of the pillow. "I'm still not exactly sure what I'm doing here." She sighed.

The last thing she remembered after the gunshots came through her wall and Justin dragged her to the floor, was the two of them crawling to, then jumping out the back window of her apartment to the fire escape. The rest was just a blur. Somehow, Justin had hustled her to the far end of the parking lot where he'd left his motorcycle. Then, without so much as a backward glance, absconded with her into the night. He hadn't even given her time to pack her toothbrush. Not that she'd left anything that couldn't be replaced, but it would have been nice to pack a few toiletries before leaping to safety.

And now she was here. Alone. With Justin. Wearing nothing but his shirt. What was wrong with this picture? Perhaps part of the problem was that—until tonight anyway—they had never even liked each other.

Very curious.

"You must be joking," Justin said as he carried a small tray holding three steaming TV dinners and two frosty cans of soda into the living room. Setting the tray before her on the coffee table, Justin straightened and looked her in the eye. "You can't tell me that you would have spent the night there. Not with that gun battle going on next door."

Patsy's smile was rueful. "Probably not. I'm glad you had the presence of mind to get us out of there safely. If you hadn't shown up I don't know what would have happened."

His cheeks puffing as he exhaled, Justin shook his head and lowered himself to the couch beside her. "No telling.

At any rate, you're welcome to stay here as long as you like. Friends tell me that this sofa is pretty comfy." He patted the cushions.

"Couldn't be any worse than the bed I've been sleeping on for the last two months." Smiling, she looked up at him and was filled with gratitude. If it hadn't been for Justin, she might not be alive right now. "Thank you for your offer to stay," she murmured.

"I mean it. My couch is your couch for as long as you need it."

Her heart hammered as she caught a flicker of flirtation in Justin's eyes. Averting her gaze, she cleared her throat. "And thank you for cooking." She gestured to the food. "It looks delicious."

Justin chuckled. "I wouldn't really call it cooking, but it will have to do."

He passed her a fork and, being ravenous, Patsy dug in with enthusiasm.

"Gun fighting agrees with you," he teased, watching her eat with interest.

"I hope you have several more of these," she said, rolling her eyes rapturously. "Where do you get them? I've never had anything like it."

"TV dinners?" Justin grinned and shook his head. "You can find 'em in the freezer section at the grocery store."

"Really? I'll have to stock up. They're wonderful."

"They come in different flavors…" he said, watching as she polished off the Salisbury steak and headed for the spuds.

"No kidding? What a concept! I love it. We always had to dress for dinner at my house when I was a kid. It was a drag."

"That's hard to imagine."

Patsy stopped eating for a moment, once she'd realized

her faux pas. "Oh. Gosh. I'm really sorry. I bet you think I'm an ungrateful wretch."

"No."

The expression on his face was sweet. Sincere. Patsy sighed with relief. "Well, anyway, these are great."

"My TV dinners are your TV dinners."

"Mmm. Thank you. I promise not to eat you out of house and home. I want to find my own place," she mumbled around a mouthful of mashed potatoes and gravy. "As soon as possible. I need to prove to Big Daddy that I'm capable of making it on my own."

"Surely your father wouldn't hold it against you if you needed to depend on a friend to get out of a bad situation."

He was beginning to consider her a friend? Little tingles of pleasure trickled down her spine. It had been a long time since she'd had someone she could truly call a friend.

"No, he wouldn't. But Justin," she explained, "I need to prove it to *me*."

After looking at her for a long and hard moment, Justin finally gave his head a slow nod. "I understand."

Patsy beamed. He did. She could tell.

"Which reminds me. I forgot to tell you about my little—" he frowned and took a sip from his can "—conversation with Bitsy."

"Oh! That's right! In all the excitement, I completely forgot about her. What's the story?"

"You're dancing on Saturday night at the party."

Patsy's fork dangled between her fingertips. *"What?"*

Justin cleared his throat, and glanced uncomfortably around the room before his gaze came to rest on hers. "What can I say? You were right. The woman is a verbal steamroller." He shrugged. "Besides, I was busy being shot at. I didn't have time to explain your little…prank."

"Ohhh," Patsy groaned. "I can't believe it. Give me your phone. I'll call her right now."

His expression was sheepish. "It's, uh, too late."

"What are you talking about? It's not even ten yet."

"The committee meeting is most likely over."

"The committee meeting? What committee meeting?"

Justin chewed his lower lip, and grimaced. "The one that sewed up all the…final details. She faxed the newspapers over an hour ago."

"You're kidding," she said hopefully.

"I wish I were. They are all, uh, well, they're all pretty excited about having you."

"Well I would be, too!" Patsy ranted. "It's not often a member of a world-famous dance troupe puts on a show for the locals."

"You wrote that you danced for a world-famous dance team?" His eyes widened.

Patsy clapped a palm over her forehead, a tortured moan emanating from deep in her throat. "I may have alluded to an Irish-type dance tour, yes…*ohhh*…" she groaned pitifully, cradling her head now in her hands. "I don't know! I can't remember if I erased that part or not! Oh good grief!" She peered up at him through her fingers. "How could you have let her do this to me?"

"Sorry…"

"Oh my gosh. Oh…my…gosh. Oh my gosh!" Patsy groaned, and pushed her plate away. "I wish the neighbors would have shot me."

Justin grinned at her theatrics. "Oh, and there's one more thing…"

"Don't tell me," she moaned, covering her face with the pillow that had been in her lap.

"You have to bring your husband and kids."

"My *husband and kids?*" she shrieked. Yanking the pillow from her face she stared at him through bleary eyes.

"The…uh, talented and gifted ones." He bit back a grin.

Eyes narrowed, Patsy squinted at him. He was enjoying

this. Jumping to her knees, she hiked the afghan around her waist and pointed an accusatory finger at him. "You did this on purpose!"

"No! I didn't. Honest." Hands up, he crossed his heart and showed her two fingers, Boy Scout style.

She'd dealt with Bitsy before. She believed him. Flopping over the couch's back, she let loose with a guttural cry that sounded as if she had indeed just been shot. *Oh, this just…just…just…* stunk! Her hair brushed the floor below, and for a moment, she pondered tearing it out by the roots.

"Where in the *heck,*" she muttered brokenly, "am I going to get a *husband* and *two* talented and gifted *children* in less than a month?" Slowly, pulling herself upright, hair flying, eyes wild, her gaze settled on Justin.

His face fell.

Justin would never know how he'd allowed himself to get talked into this debacle. Without a doubt, it was the most insane thing he'd ever agreed to.

He was no jogger, for crying in the night.

He was an instructor at a ranch for wayward children. Slapping off the alarm clock, he squinted at the glowing LED numbers. Five a.m. On Sunday, no less. Next to spending the day on the operating table having his appendix removed with a rusty hacksaw, jogging was one of his least favorite hobbies. Unless of course he had a football tucked under his arm, and a passel of screaming kids hot on his heels.

Unfortunately jogging was only the tip of the iceberg, he realized, and his stomach sank even further as yesterday's dismal conversation with Patsy came flooding back. Throwing back the covers, he plunged his hands through his hair and groaned. Last night before they'd turned in, Patsy had somehow commandeered him into not only acting as her training coach—but posing as her husband at the reunion as well.

He rolled his sleepy eyes and flopped back on his bed. From what dementia had he been suffering when he'd buckled to her harebrained schemes? Had he really promised to help her out by pretending to be a surgeon at her ten-year reunion? He seemed to remember making a feeble attempt at talking his way out of this travesty, but she'd fixed those limpid baby blues on him at a weak moment, and he'd been a goner. Besides. He had to admit. He'd been to blame for at least part of her predicament. And, she needed his help. Plus, being his future partner's sister, he felt more obligated to her than perhaps he normally would have in other circumstances. Buck and Holly had been very good to him. The least he could do was help bail their sister out of this jam.

So. Now he was not only her significant other, but he was her fitness coach as well. Had he lost his blasted mind?

It didn't seem to matter one whit to Patsy that he'd saved her life that evening. Oh, no. As far as Patsy was concerned, she'd rather have been put down by the neighborhood firing squad. At least then she'd have had a plausible excuse to keep from getting up in front of an audience in her "shape." And, she'd—in a most wifely fashion—informed him, if she had to suffer her way back into shape, then by golly, he did, too.

Justin had protested that she looked to be in wonderful shape. It was true, he thought, his pulse thrumming in his ears as he lay staring through the morning shadows at his ceiling. To him she looked far better than he had any right to think his boss's sister looked. However, to his flattering comment about her wonderful shape, Patsy had simply snorted and observed that he knew very little about dance.

Shaking his head to clear it of the cobwebs, Justin pushed himself upright on the bed. Then, he stood and rummaged through a dresser drawer and emerged with a pair of running shorts and a T-shirt. As he stumbled around in the darkness, he could hear Patsy already rustling around in the living room, getting ready for their "jogging date." Once he'd dragged a comb through his hair and a toothbrush through his mouth, he headed to the kitchen to make coffee.

"We don't have time for that," Patsy informed him from over his shoulder. "Besides, it's best to jog on caffeine-free beverages, such as water."

Justin stared blurrily at her. "You're kidding." Man, she looked good in the morning.

She grinned, perky and obviously raring to go. "Nope."

"Okay, fine." He bent low and rummaged through his lower cabinets for an omelet pan. "Just give me a few seconds to whip us up a little breakfast."

"None for me, honey bun," Patsy said, obviously jovial now that her reunion problems were all but solved.

"Why not?" Justin turned and stared at her in exasperation.

"Jogging on a full stomach makes me sick." Lifting a delicate shoulder, she continued. "Besides, I need to lose at least ten pounds over the next few weeks."

"Ten pounds?" Grabbing a loaf of bread, Justin stuffed two pieces into the toaster and stared at her. Ten pounds? Was she serious? "In just a few weeks? Why?"

"Because I'm fat. That's why."

"In the head, maybe." He nodded. "Everywhere else..." As the bread began to toast, he eyed her with an appreciative glance. She looked about as toned as one could get, standing there in her cutoff sweatpants and torn-up T-shirt. "...I'd have to say you're just about right."

Patsy colored girlishly. "No. You don't understand. In dance you have to be perfect. I've let myself go for over a year now. I'm soft."

"So what's wrong with that?" Justin couldn't keep the prurient interest from his voice.

She sighed heavily. "Granted, I'm probably still in better shape than the average bear, but I have a long way to go before I can get up in front of all my old classmates and put on a show, that's for sure."

"Whatever," Justin mumbled and poured himself a glass of milk. "I just don't get why we have to get up at this ungodly hour of the morning."

"Because it's the best time to go. Before the sun comes up and it gets, you know, all—" she flapped her delicate hands and pulled a cute face "—hot and bothered."

Five a.m. and she was a living doll. Pretending to be her husband would be far more interesting than it should be, he knew. Looking at her right now, he knew why he'd capitulated. She was irresistible. Justin attempted to swallow.

"Hot and bothered," he repeated dully.

Unable to stop himself, Justin allowed his eyes to roam the curves that had been flitting through his dreams last night. It boggled his mind. She wanted to get up in the middle of the night and run over hill and dale in Hidden Valley until she lost ten pounds? Good heavens, there would be nothing left of her. She was perfect just the way she was. He'd never liked overly skinny women. Darlene had been as shapely as a rake and nearly as much fun to hug.

"Yeah," Patsy continued, looking longingly at the strawberry jelly he was in the process of slathering on his toast. "We'll get hot and sweaty enough going early."

"Sweaty." Justin took a calming breath.

"Mmm-hmm." Her translucent blue eyes flitted expectantly to his.

Why hadn't he ever noticed how strikingly beautiful her eyes were before last night? The most unusual sky blue light shimmered in these two reflective pools, unlike anything he'd ever seen. They could render him incapable of rational thought with a single glance. Slowly he chewed his toast and studied this hardheaded debutante-waif in fascination.

"Patsy," he began, backhanding his mouth to rid it of traces of his breakfast. His heart was skipping beats in a most alarming way. Vaguely he wondered if he was up to this jogging thing with such a distracting woman. It wouldn't do to have a coronary out in the middle of nowhere with only Patsy to doctor him. Obviously—by the way she'd managed to ignore her derelict neighbors—she didn't have a real tight handle on reality and the emergencies that could crop up from time to time. Perhaps he could talk her out of jogging altogether.

"I really, really don't think it's a good idea for you to lose ten pounds. I mean, come on, on you, losing that much weight would be dangerous. Besides, I'm not kidding when I tell you that you look great, just the way you are."

She lifted her eyes to his and smiled bashfully. "Thanks, but you haven't seen me naked."

Justin's Adam's apple danced and bobbed, threatening to choke him. He tugged at the neck of his T-shirt.

"Seriously," she continued, completely oblivious to the effect her words had on him, and glanced past her full bustline to the curve of her hips, "if I could lose ten pounds, I'll probably regain a little of the cardiovascular shape I'll need for a dance routine. Plus, I was voted most likely to succeed. It's important that I look successful."

Justin tossed a beleaguered glance toward the heavens, shrugged and gulped down the last of his milk. "Okay. Whatever." This need to impress other people by still being the most likely to succeed after all this time, was lost on him, but if it meant that much to her, then he guessed he'd simply have to suffer along. After all, she was his future partner's sister. He owed her.

By the time they'd run the mile it took to reach the outskirts of Hidden Valley, Justin was finally awake and hitting his stride. It was amazing, considering that sleep hadn't come easy last night. It had finally arrived in restless fits and starts, and all because he hadn't been able to clear the haunting feeling of Patsy's arms wrapped tightly around his waist as they'd sped home on his motorcycle last night.

Man, he thought, wiping the side of his face on the shoulder of his T-shirt as they slogged over hill and dale, he'd have to figure out a way to get her back on his motorcycle. Soon.

"Hey, Brubaker," he called over his shoulder, slowing a beat to wait for her to catch up. She was beginning to lose steam. He grinned.

Somewhere he'd heard that a person should be able to carry on a conversation while they ran. Supposedly it was a good way to tell if you were going too fast. Might as well test the theory on the wilting lily now. Besides, Justin decided, some conversation might make this boring jogging business a little more palatable.

"Huh?" she puffed. As they arrived at a crosswalk, Patsy clutched a signpost, mopped her brow with the hem of her T-shirt and waited for the light to change.

"Having fun?"

Patsy nodded and panted. "Oh, yeah. This is great."

"It really is, huh? I have to admit, I'm enjoying it much more than I thought I would." Justin smiled as he took in the patches of fire on her cheeks. The hair at the sides of her head was plastered down, damp with her exertion. Yes, this was a barrel of monkeys.

"Great." Turning toward him, she stumbled over a crack in the sidewalk and caught herself on his arm just before her knees buckled. "I really need this. This will really help me get back into shape," she assured him.

"In that case, I can't wait until tomorrow morning."

Patsy blanched, then quickly recovered. "Uh, yeah. Great."

With a wide grin, Justin tossed her the conversational ball. "Have you given any thought to what kind of research I should be doing on my role as Dr. Oscar Madison? I had my tonsils out when I was a kid, but that's about the extent of my medical expertise."

"Cute." Still gasping for oxygen, she squinted up at him.

The light changed, their cue to cross the intersection. With great interest, Justin watched Patsy grip her side as she ventured into the street.

"Well," she said breathily, "we can watch some medical shows in the evening. 'ER' and, uh, maybe some old 'Emergency' reruns should be helpful. They are always saying stuff like 'Give me an IV drip!' and 'Give me five cc's of Ringer's lactate, stat…'"

"I'll remember those things when I'm ordering a drink at the reunion," he quipped.

"Funny…*ahhhh*," she moaned, slowing slightly.

"What's wrong?"

"Just…a…stitch. Don't…worry. It'll go…*oowwway*." She waved a nonchalant hand, her smile a brittle grimace. Inhaling deep breaths against the pain, Patsy doggedly moved toward the opposite curb, matching her stride the best she could to his.

"Patsy, we could stop if you want," Justin suggested, concerned at the way she was wincing with each labored breath. "We could take a cab home."

"No!"

"Why not? You don't look so good."

"I'm fine," she lied. "Ask any dancer. You have to go through a lot of pain to get into top condition."

"Well, we don't have to traverse the entire continent this morning," he griped. "After all, this is our first day." Hopefully it would be their last, he thought, longing for a steaming cup of coffee. Patsy didn't look too good. Maybe he could talk her into resting up at yonder Starbucks.

"I know, but we…*oww*…don't have…*ooo*…much time left and I need…to do this if I'm going to be able to dance…"

He rolled his eyes. So much for his morning cup of Java.

She bared her teeth at him, and Justin couldn't be sure if she was smiling at—or threatening—him. Shaking his head at her stubborn pride, he continued trotting along, allowing her to set the pace.

"You know, Justin," she puffed, still clutching the stitch in her side, "I have an idea about…*uhgg,* the dance thing I'm doing."

"Mmm?" Justin asked, trying to keep his mind on the task at hand rather than the fetching picture Patsy made, her firm legs pounding over the pavement, wisps of hair sliding free from her ponytail. No matter how undesirable he found jogging at the crack of dawn to be, he was beginning to see a certain charm in the habit.

"I was thinking maybe I'd have some of the kids from my dancing class come with me—the ones that aren't pregnant, of course—since I think Bitsy is expecting a number of dancers."

Justin frowned at her as he trotted along. "She is?"

"Uh, yeah, uh, I've been thinking about it, and I'm pretty sure I forgot to erase the part about the Irish dance tour…" A pained expression crossed her face, and Justin couldn't tell if it was from the jogging or from the questionnaire that had been inadvertently mailed to Bitsy.

"Oh, boy," he muttered under his breath. He could just

see Patsy's motley crew trying to pass for a professional team.

Seemingly undaunted, Patsy continued to brainstorm. "I, uh, uh, thought we could do a Christmas pageant-type number…"

The sun was finally beginning to send the first tentative rays of sunlight into the little valley where they ran on the suburban streets. They slowed down as they came to another crosswalk, and though the light was green, Patsy fell against the pole and gasped for oxygen. Bending over, she clutched her shirt and mopped her profusely sweating face, and prayed she wouldn't keel over from a heat stroke. Perhaps they should take it just a tad slower, she mused, pulling the now soaking shirt away from her face and catching Justin's interested stare at her bare midsection.

Guiltily his gaze shot to hers. "What's wrong? Your side hurting?"

"Yeah. A little." Everything hurt. At this rate, she should be in shape to dance in three—maybe two, if she was lucky—years.

"Take a deep breath," Justin advised, "then let it all the way out. Then, breathe in shallow, breathe out deep. Keep doing that. It should help."

"Yeah, yeah, I know the drill. Really, it's just a stitch. I've had them before." But never to this intensity. Could one year of debauchery really deteriorate one's conditioning so dramatically? She hadn't suffered this much physical pain since her early dance days in Europe. It was amazing what damage day after day of floating in a pool and eating comfort foods could do to the dancer's body.

Looking both ways, he waved to her. "Well, okay, come on, let's get this over with."

Patsy wanted to slug him as he cruised along so effortlessly. He hadn't even broken a sweat yet, and here she was, sucking wind like a clogged Hoover. And *she* was the professional athlete. Sort of.

"Well, anyway, if the kids agree to perform with me...*eeessshhh*—" she gripped her side "—that could solve some of my problems. One of these days, I'll stop at the video store and rent one of those Irish dance videos. Maybe there are some simple steps I could teach the kids."

"Worth a try. You can watch the video on my VCR, if you like."

"Thank*ssss*." She must sound as if she'd been inhaling helium, she thought, chagrined.

"Are you sure you're all right?"

"*Eeeyesss*," she hissed, willing herself toward some imaginary finish line. "Justin," she began, striving to ignore the pains that squeezed the breath from her lungs.

"Hmm?"

"I've been thinking..."

"Uh-oh."

"About us being married, and you know, acting that way."

Justin quirked a rakish brow.

"Not that kind of thinking."

"Aww. Too bad."

She whapped him with an impatient hand. "We are going...to have to rehearse...our relationship a little bit."

"We are?"

"Yep. And, spend...some time...strategizing. Getting to know each other, so that no one will ask a bunch...of questions that will leave us...unprepared."

"You mean like, 'Hey, Patsy, does Dr. Oscar sleep in the nude?' That kind of question?" An impish grin split his face as he easily trotted along.

"Oh, you're impossible," she huffed, the pain in her side growing worse, though she wasn't sure if it was from the jogging or Justin's irreverent teasing. Would he control himself at the reunion? "Another thing crossed my mind..."

Justin sighed. "What now?"

"Where...are we going to get two...talented and gifted kids to bring to the family picnic...on Saturday afternoon?"

"Let's bring Marky and Mikey. I have custody of them, so bringing them to a family picnic should be no problem." Justin shrugged easily. Problem solved.

"Marky and Mikey? Are you...*kidding?* They are expecting talented and gifted kids!"

"Marky and Mikey are talented."

"At picking pockets, yes."

"They'll be fine. You'll see."

Patsy sighed and forced herself to smile against the multitude of aches and pains that assailed her. Her audible moan drew Justin's eyes, and much to her eternal frustration, a brand-new searing pain began to curl around her shins as she hobbled along. Each jarring footfall across the sidewalk's pavement served only to increase the intensity of her discomfort. It was torture. She, of all people, should have known better than to go jogging without properly stretching first. If she'd only stretched out and eaten a little breakfast. Drunk a little water. Slept more than two hours. Certainly, she couldn't be *that* out of shape.

No way could she tell Justin of her embarrassing plight. He would probably say, "I told you so." And, she thought, tears of agony forming behind her eyelids, he'd be right.

"Ow...ow...ow...ow..." she chanted under her breath as she limped along.

"Enjoying yourself?" Justin asked conversationally.

"Yes, ow...this is...ow...super."

"We'd better hurry if we're going to make that next light," Justin advised, shooting a sly glance in her direction.

"Right behind you," she sang out. Biting back a sob, she forced her way across what had become a blur of excruciating pavement. Her hammering heart threatened to burst out of her rib cage as she watched Justin move ahead. Slowing, she dragged one foot after the other, and—blinking away the tears that threatened—could see his fluid figure growing smaller off in the distance.

"Help," she squeaked, trying to get his attention.

She was dying.

She wanted Justin to know. That way someone could tell Buck and Holly. And her folks. And, of course, the coroner.

"Ohhh," she moaned, unable to bear the pain any longer. Finally slowing to a stop, she crumpled into a fetal ball on someone's front lawn. A dog barked menacingly from behind the house.

Justin's easy gait carried him for half a block before he realized that Patsy was no longer limping along behind him. Stopping in his tracks, he turned to see her sprawled out on a patch of grass in front of a house. Fear rippled down his spine as he rushed back to her side. Bending low, he placed a gentle hand on her shoulder.

"Patsy?" he breathed, worry etching creases into his brow. "Patsy, are you all right?"

"Just a second," she responded brightly, through her tightly gritted teeth. Hauling herself up to her knees, she began to crawl toward the sidewalk. "I, uh, just have to get my second wind."

Exhaling heavily, Justin watched her for a moment, shaking his head. "Brubaker, stop. Listen, kiddo, you can't crawl home. We must be at least an hour away."

"Don't call me kiddo," she flung back at him, furiously. Damn. He was right. She couldn't crawl home. "Oh, Justin," she blubbered in a tortured voice as she rocked back on her blistered heels and looked up at him through bleary eyes. "What are we going to do? It hurts so bad. I don't think I can make it any farther.'' Doubling over, Patsy hid her face in her hands.

The dog snarled and growled viciously.

"Well," Justin said, raking a nervous hand over his jaw and glancing in the direction of probable canine attack. "We can't stay here."

"I know." She looked up at him, her eyes filled with pain and embarrassment. "You go on. I'll catch up later."

Justin snorted softly. "Like hell. We're at least three miles from home, not to mention the fact that Jaws over there is trying to figure out how to filet you." He pointed in the direction of the snapping dog whose head bobbed excitedly above the backyard gate. Any minute now, he'd sail over the top and rip them to shreds.

"Fine," she gasped. "It would put me out of my misery. He couldn't do anything to make it any worse. Plus," she joked in a feeble attempt at humor, "I wouldn't have to go to the reunion, if he ate me."

"Very funny. Come on," he commanded, reaching down and lifting her beneath the arms and propping her up on her rubbery legs. "We have to get out of here."

"I can't," she cried, sagging miserably against him.

"Oh, for the love of…" Justin turned around and, reaching behind him, pulled her thighs up onto his hips. "Grab on," he needlessly instructed as Patsy flopped against his back and, clutching him around the neck, hung on for dear life. "Not that tight," he said, choking.

"Sorry," she mumbled, marveling at how effortlessly he carried her piggyback-style, down the sidewalk. Why, he acted as though she was as light as a feather. His shoulders were as hard as granite, further sealing her impression of him as a marble statue. The silky hair at his nape tickled her nose as she relaxed against his virile body.

The sunrise was beginning to send dappled shadows through the trees to the sidewalk, and Patsy watched sleepily as the new day dawned. Birds chattered and one by one, folks began to emerge from their houses, decked out in their Sunday best and smiling indulgently at the young man who trotted by, carrying his ladylove on his back.

"How sweet," one woman was heard to murmur as they went by.

Patsy's blood began to sing through her veins. She'd almost be willing to take up jogging as a permanent hobby, if the result was the same as this every day. Just the sheer physical joy of feeling Justin's muscles move beneath her body would be worth every ache and pain she was sure to wake up with tomorrow morning.

Closing her eyes, Patsy sighed. This was getting to be a bad habit, Justin bailing her out of one scrape after another, this way. She buried her nose in his neck and inhaled the divinely male scent that was uniquely Justin. Mmm. A bad habit.

Enjoyable. But bad.

Chapter Six

Justin gently laid Patsy down on his couch, his body lowering down beside hers as they sank into the plush leather
cushion. Her arms still wound tightly around his neck, he
hovered at the edge of the seat and struggled to bring his
breathing under control. He was not sure if he was so oxygen deprived because he'd just trudged three miles with
her piggyback-style or if it was instead the sincere look of
gratitude swimming in the baby blues that looked so lim-
pidly up at him at the moment.

For better than an hour he'd carried Patsy, her arms
clutching his shoulders and chest, her legs wrapped tightly
around his waist and resting in the cradle of his arms. Snug-
gled against his shoulder, she'd buried her nose in the crook
of his neck and, much to his disbelief and delight, slept.
Never in his entire life had he felt more possessive over
another human being.

Shivers of something wonderful had zigzagged down his
spine as her light breathing fanned his nape. The heat of
her body gave off a warm, spicy scent that made him want

to gobble her up like a sleeping gingerbread-man, fresh out of the oven.

She'd been as light as a child, slumped with sleep. It was only three miles from the suburbs back to the ranch. However, he'd have gladly walked across the country with her that day, so much did he enjoy the feeling of her lithe body pressed against his.

Something about Patsy Brubaker was getting under his skin in a big way. This took him by surprise, as he'd been so sure he'd nicely pigeonholed her from the beginning, and could now avoid her without trouble.

Unfortunately his ability to avoid her was rapidly becoming a thing of the past.

"Are you going to be okay?" he murmured, wondering if she could hear his thundering heart straining to burst free from his chest. His nose hovered just slightly above hers, and she showed no signs of releasing her grip on his neck.

Wincing, she pulled her bottom lip between her teeth and stretched slightly, as if testing the extent of her injuries. "Mmm-hmm. Yeah," she whispered. "I think I'll be fine." Her eyes flashed as they searched his. "Thanks to you."

"No problem."

A teasing light sparked in her eyes. "When we get to the reunion, I'll let you call me the 'old-ball-and-chain,' if you want."

Justin chuckled. Her fingers toyed absently with the hair at his nape, sending jolts of electricity rippling between his shoulder blades. His voice was rough and rather unsteady in his ears. "I'm, ah, beginning to think married life won't be as bad as all that..."

Patsy's lips tipped up at the corners.

He arched a rakish brow and the sands of time stopped sifting through the hourglass for a moment. It would be so easy to kiss her, he thought, as her sweet, warm breath caressed his cheeks. The scent of his shampoo and deodorant on her delicate skin was soft and fragrant from the shower she'd taken in his bathroom last night. The blood that roared in his ears picked up in tempo at the thought of her all steamy and wet from the shower. Kind of like she was now, only wearing a towel. Without a speck of makeup, she was a raving beauty, unlike the heavily sprayed, coiffed and powdered Darlene.

Justin stilled as he studied the beauty beneath him. As Patsy lay so serenely looking back at him, he could tell that she had no idea that a hurricane of desire was suddenly sweeping him over. Her full lips lay a hairsbreadth from his own, and he gritted his teeth to keep himself from doing something stupid like pressing his mouth to hers.

Pressing his body to hers...

Loosening the clasp that held her ponytail at the top of her head, and filling his hands with the spun gold he found there...

That would be stupid.

Really stupid, he thought, as he reached out with the back of his forefinger and traced the smooth lines of her cheek. Her jaw. Her heart-shaped chin. The classic Brubaker dimples that parenthesized the corners of her rosy lips. Bringing the pad of his thumb to her lower lip, he traced its fullness and then, sliding his hand lower, cupped his fingers at the side of her neck. Slowly he stretched out the full length of the couch next to her, and drew her inexorably toward him.

He heard her sharp intake of breath, and was suddenly lost in the churning sea of her blue eyes. For a moment his face was suspended over hers, poised, waiting. The ceiling fan whirred overhead, sending a refreshing breeze down over their heated flesh.

Pulling back, Justin searched her face for some sign of resistance or objection. When he found none, he leaned forward and touched his mouth to hers. Her hands tightened their grasp at the back of his head.

And that was all the encouragement he needed to commit what would surely be one of the most stupid mistakes of his life.

They would never be able to undo this, once it was done. Forever, after this moment, there would be this kiss between them.

Everything would change.

As her mouth moved tentatively beneath his, the past, present and future flashed before his eyes. No longer would he simply be Buck's friend and potential business partner. No. Now there would be a bond, of sorts, between Patsy and himself that could never be overlooked. No matter how much they might wish to in the future.

Pushing this niggling worry to the back of his mind, he settled his lips firmly over hers, and feeling her pulse quicken beneath his touch at her throat, gently encouraged her response. The CD that had been playing lightly on his stereo ended, and a new one began. A groan, most likely coming from the depths of his churning gut, vibrated into his throat as he pushed her mouth open with his own. The feel of her mouth, fitting so perfectly with his, sent his fiery blood surging through his body like a flash fire, as their kiss became more heated. An answering shiver radiated from her body, and he pressed closer, covering her upper body with his. Planes and curves came together, here and there, as Justin reached up and pulled the clasp from Patsy's hair, freeing it, filling his hands with waves of incredible softness and light.

Suddenly he didn't need oxygen to sustain himself. Not when he had Patsy's kiss. He didn't need sunshine. Not when he had the warmth of her arms. He didn't need any earthly fortification. Not when he'd found heaven with Patsy.

Cradling her face in his hands, he kissed her until they were both senseless with yearning. As he angled her head, he breathlessly tore his mouth from hers and burned a trail of kisses from her jaw to the hollow of her throat, and her breathing became ragged, heavy.

He wanted her more than he'd ever wanted anything else in his sadly lacking life. He needed her. Craved her. The way he used to crave a close relationship with a family of his own as a kid. Suddenly Justin realized that he was beginning to grow attached to her. Like a tree that needed fertile ground in which to flourish, Justin was becoming attached to Patsy.

What in thunder was he thinking? he wondered, feeling suddenly panicky as he buried his face into her hair. He was getting too close to this woman. Their lives were galaxies apart. It could never work out between them. For crying in the night, he was making the same mistake all over again.

This was not good.

For more reasons than she simply reminded him of Darlene. Although the comparisons were growing weaker as he got to know her better. But even so, he had no business getting all hot and bothered by his future business partner's younger sister. It was bad for business. It was bad for his relationship with her brother. It was bad for his blood pressure.

He wasn't really her husband. He had to get that through his thick skull.

With a superhuman effort that required more strength than it would have taken to carry Patsy Brubaker across Texas, Justin tore himself from her embrace. He pushed himself up on the couch, and her arms slid from his shoulders over his chest. As he brought himself to his feet, he stood, his hands planted firmly at his hips, and looked down at her. The boss's younger sister. Mentally he called himself every kind of fool.

Lying motionless, a wounded look flashing briefly in her eyes, Patsy watched him.

Many moments passed as they stared at each other, trying to come to grips with what had just transpired. Trying to figure out how they were going to act around each other now. Trying to pretend it wasn't at all unusual for them to tussle on his couch at the crack of dawn on any given Sunday.

Justin dragged a hand through his hair, and over his beard-roughened chin, as emotions went to war in his belly. Flexing his fists, he wondered what had happened to the Justin that used to live here. The independent guy. The private guy. The guy who had sworn off women that were too rich for his blood. Obviously some bozo had invaded his body and robbed him of his senses.

Patsy righted herself to a seated position and smoothed her untamed mop of curls away from her face.

Smiling brightly, it was obvious she was doing her best to blink away her hurt and confusion at his sudden rejection. She clasped her hands tightly together in her lap. Chin tipped, she effected a practiced air of poise and sophistication.

The vibes in the room had changed color, then died, as surely as the leaves of autumn.

As Patsy's gaze wandered to the wall clock, Justin's followed. Slowly his eyes slid closed. Not yet seven a.m. and the day stretched out like a Texas freeway. His gaze shifted back to Patsy. What the heck were they going to do now?

"Well now," Patsy said in a clipped tone, her voice unusually businesslike in the hush of the early morning, "we should probably get to work."

Aw, damn, Justin thought, completely disgusted with himself. She was back to being the prickly pear that had shown up to interview in her dance togs two months ago. They had returned to square one, it would seem, and were as awkward as freshly hatched vultures around each other once more. Just when he was getting to know the real Patsy Brubaker.

He inhaled deeply, then blew slowly out. "It's Sunday."

"Oh…oh." She colored as the realization dawned. "Um, well then. Of course you have plans…so…I should probably be on my way to you know, church…" She tugged and smoothed her rumpled sweats as if she didn't have a care in the world. Least of all, him.

"You…uh—" he cleared his throat and continued "—I mean I don't have any plans today." Pausing, he frowned slightly and wondered what had possessed him to admit that. She'd given him the perfect out. Why hadn't he taken it? He could definitely use the time away from this tennis shoe-clad temptation to get his head together.

"Oh, no. You don't have to baby-sit me. I can just, you know—" she waved an airy hand "—go sit outside and wait for Buck and Holly to wake up…"

"Don't be ridiculous," he snapped, irritated at her imperious tone.

Patsy lifted a finely arched brow. "Now I'm ridiculous."

Boy, he was certainly digging himself a fine hole. He sighed.

"What I mean is, Marky and Mikey are going to Buck and Holly's this morning."

Marky and Mikey slept with eight other little boys and their counselor in the bunkhouse behind Justin's trailer. Most days, he'd roust those two out of bed, and do something special with them, but this morning, they had plans of their own. "They are going to help some of the other kids bake pies and cookies for the Thanksgiving dinner that we've been planning here at the ranch dining room. So…I'm on my own until this afternoon."

"Oh." She sniffed.

"Are you going?"

"Yes, I really should be on my way," she announced, leaping to her feet and straightening a pile of afghans that lay in a tangle at the end of the couch. Once she had completed her task, she spun around to face him.

Justin pulled his grin between his teeth. "Not now. I meant, are you going to attend the Thanksgiving dinner here at the ranch this coming Thursday?"

Taken back, she blinked up at him. "Oh. Well. I...hadn't really thought about the holidays yet. My mother and Big Daddy are spending Thanksgiving and Christmas in New England with my mother's side of the family." Her shoulders jumped and her eyes darted to her hands. "They invited me, but I can't afford to go." She tossed her head defiantly. "And I refuse to take handouts from my dad."

"In that case, maybe you should talk to Buck about spending Thanksgiving here at the ranch." He shot her an offhand glance. Now the idiot that had invaded his body was inventing excuses to spend more time with her. "We could use the help."

"Uh, well I guess, with such a delightful, heartfelt invitation, I mean, how can I refuse?" she intoned sarcastically. She sent her eyes flitting around the room, avoiding his gaze.

"Hey, listen," Justin said and passed a frustrated hand across his forehead, "I didn't mean it the way it sounded."

"Sure."

"No, really. I just..." Squeezing his eyes tightly shut, he groped for the proper wording. "We're going to be spending a lot of time together getting ready for this reunion thing...and I...I'm not ready for a serio..."

"Hey, it doesn't take a brick house to fall on me," Patsy said, her forced laughter ringing hollow. "I get it. You don't want it to get too personal..."

"No, that's not…"

"That's fine," she continued, not listening, steamrolling ahead, saving her pride.

"It is?"

"Yes, I don't want it to get too personal between us, either." The look on her delicate face was pained, as if she'd come in contact with something unseemly out in the dumpster.

"You don't?" He crossed his arms over his chest. He felt as if he'd just been slapped.

"Right. I think that we should try to keep this whole reunion thing to just what it is."

"And, just what is it, exactly?" Justin demanded, growing hot under the collar. Nothing pushed his buttons the way a woman with an upper-crust attitude problem could.

Patsy paused and considered. "A professional relationship."

"Professional?" He snorted, and took a step toward her. What had just happened between them there on his couch was hardly what he would call professional behavior. Whether she admitted it or not, she had wanted him, just as much as he had wanted her.

"Yes." She frowned uncertainly. "Uh, here at work, we are, you know, co-workers. You stay in your corner, and I'll stay in mine, whenever we're—" she glanced nervously around the room "—alone. As far as I'm concerned what just happened was simply a practice session, and nothing more. Let's just forget it, okay? I mean, you don't have to go overboard on this thing. When it comes to the reunion, you are simply going to be my rented groom."

Justin swallowed. *Overboard? Practice session?* Was she serious?

"Yeah, right. Don't you think your classmates will suspect something is amiss in paradise if we act as if I'm simply doing you a favor, *darling?*'' He knew his voice was bordering on the snide, but couldn't help it.

A pink flush crept up her face and into her cheeks and, reaching down, she snatched her hair clip off the floor where he'd tossed it in the heat of passion. Making a big production out of twisting her wild curls into a ponytail at the top of her head, she averted his gaze.

"Well, of course," she snapped churlishly, "there will be times…when we will have to show affection…in public, so…I suppose it's, you know, uh, good that we worked a few of the kinks out just now."

Watching her balletic movements as she gracefully tied up her hair, Justin decided that if that were the case, then he wanted to work out a few more kinks before they debuted at the reunion. Now was as good a time as any.

"Of course." He grinned at the identical candy apple spots on her cheeks as she finally secured her flyaway hair. "Just to set the record straight, why don't we go over exactly what kind of affection you expect from me in…public? Just so there won't be any misunderstandings."

Dropping her arms, she huffed, exasperated. "Must I spell it out for you?"

Lashes at half-mast, he eyed her and then took another step forward. He was standing mere inches from her. "I'm not much at spelling. How about a demonstration?"

Flustered, her breathing picked up. "It doesn't take a rocket scientist to figure out how to hold my hand," she testily informed him.

"Lucky thing you're a rocket scientist," he said drolly, reminding her of her references to NASA on the reunion questionnaire.

Her eyes flitted to his hands. "Oh, for heaven's sake," she snapped. "When the time comes, just hold my blasted hand."

"Like this?" Reaching out, he grasped her slender hands and tugged her body up against his. With their hands clasped between their bodies, Justin, a half smile on his mouth, searched Patsy's face with curious eyes.

"I...I suppose so..." She blinked.

"And, correct me if I'm wrong, but they'd probably expect to see me put my arm around your waist now and then."

"*Wellll*, I suppose. Probably."

Slowly Justin released her hands, and slipped his arms around her waist. "And, I'm just guessing here, but I suspect they wouldn't be shocked by a hug?"

"No..." Her voice was breathy in his ears.

Pulling her into his embrace, he held her close, and inhaled the intoxicating scent of her that was already permanently imprinted on his brain. The clip that held her hair fell to the floor again, as he released it and filled his hands with her soft waves. Tilting her head back, he angled her face just beneath his, and looked into the deep blue sky of her eyes. "Friends?" he whispered against the fullness of her lips.

Her eyes slid closed as she nodded, a mixed expression of relief and apology flashing across her face. "Yes. Good. Of course. Friends," she whispered into his mouth.

"Just reviewing our practice session," he murmured before settling his mouth over hers. Nudging her lips open with his, he kissed her hard, and with a passion that would leave them both reeling for the rest of the day.

"Good job," he breathed and gave his head a clearing shake. "That ought to fool 'em."

Setting her away from him and bounding to the kitchen before he decided to throw her back on the couch and pick up where they'd left off. "I'm starving," he called to her, as she stood bewildered, staring after him, frustration radiating from her in a nearly palpable way. "How about an omelet?" Pans rattling, he disappeared beneath the counter.

Patsy rolled her eyes. "Fine." She scowled and, spinning on her heel, headed for the shower.

"Knock, knock." Justin's voice reached Patsy as she put away the last of her meager towel collection in the bathroom linen closet of her new home.

Earlier, after they'd scarfed down giant omelets, several slices of toast and an entire pot of coffee back at his place, Justin had taken Patsy over to her old apartment so that she could gather her personal belongings and give notice to the landlord. Then, after he'd taken her back to the ranch, he returned to the apartment complex with a couple of the older boys to see about getting her dumpy station wagon running and moved over to her new place.

And now, he was back.

It was after noon now, and even though it had been hours since their fateful kiss, the mere sound of his voice had the power to turn her insides to molten lava.

"Come on in, I'm back here," she called, trying to sound unaffected, and as if she were nothing but his buddy. That's the way he wanted it, and by golly, that's the way it would be. No matter how attracted to him she may be.

Wiping her cheeks on her apron, she glanced in the bathroom mirror for a quick appraisal. The rag towel she'd wrapped around her head would have to go, as would the oversize bright yellow rubber gloves. She could hear Justin climbing up her front steps and the sound of her ratty screen door falling shut behind him.

Quickly she yanked off the gloves, tossed off her towel, fluffed her hair and ran a streak of lipstick over her lower lip. Pressing her lips together, she arranged her face into her best "I'm your little buddy" expression, and pretended fascination with scrubbing the rust ring that circled her sink's drain.

The trailer next to Justin's had been everything Buck and Holly had promised, cobwebs and all. When she'd approached her brother and sister-in-law earlier that day about temporarily living in the empty apartment, they'd been more than happy to give her a key and their blessings. They both agreed that having someone live there would keep the place clean and rodent free. Patsy wasn't so sure about the possibility of small, furry roommates, but having little other choice, promised to do her best. After all, anything had to be better than being shot at through the walls.

Not much possibility of that here. Unless she counted the water pistols that Marky and Mikey were using to stage a mock shoot-out at the OK Corral just outside her window right now.

Strains of hilarity and punch-drunk giggling by children wired on sugar-cookie dough reached her ears as Justin's footsteps ambled down her hall. She smiled. The light-hearted sounds of laughter and love were what Holly and Buck had worked so hard for over the past three years. In the two short months she'd worked here and been involved with children—children with troubles the likes of which she could never have imagined in her own youth—she had fallen a little bit in love with this place. She had begun to see why Buck and Holly had left the trappings of wealth, luxury and celebrity, for the trappings of health, laughter and love.

Every day, she was able to understand Justin just a little bit better.

And, admire him just a little bit more.

"Wow." Justin's deep, sexy voice reached her as he turned the corner and discovered her scrubbing the bathroom sink. "This place sure looks a heck of a lot better.

"Mmm," she hummed, her heart hammering as she pretended to do great battle with the rust. Angling her head, she shot him a thousand-watt "Hey, buddy!" smile and continued to scrub. "Well, there's a lot to do." *Don't worry. I'll be too busy to drag you to the couch and force you to kiss me against your will,* she thought, her cheeks catching fire with her exertion. Or embarrassment. She couldn't be sure.

"Listen, I've got news," he continued, moving behind her and into the bathroom. Throwing back the moldy shower curtain, he stepped into the shower and folded his arms across his impressive chest.

Patsy watched him in the cracked mirror of her medicine cabinet as he made himself comfortable against her shower wall. She swallowed. *He was in her shower! Aaauughhh!* A herd of wild mustangs pranced and galloped through her stomach.

"Yes?" she squeaked, and began furiously scrubbing her sink once more.

"I finally got your car started."

"Oh?" *Ohhh!* She sighed, her heart doing a pirouette. He was so capable. If he could get that old wreck running, he could do anything.

"Yeah."

Lifting her eyes to the mirror, she gazed at him. His smile reminded her of the kind, sympathetic smile a doctor wore when they had to deliver bad news. "What is it?" she wondered, propping her arms on the sink and looking into the mirror.

"Wellll." He lifted a broad shoulder and grimaced. "We managed to get her over here, but that old gal is going to need some work. Especially if we are going to have to take it to the reunion. I'd offer to drive us, but I only have the motorcycle, and we wouldn't have room for all the kids. And—" he arched a philosophical brow "—I have a feel-

ing Buck and Holly won't be able to spare the van for three days right in the middle of the holidays.''

"Uh-oh," Patsy groaned and hung her head. "What are we going to do? I don't have the kind of money 'it would take to fix that old bucket of bolts.''

"I can do the work," he volunteered with an easy shrug. "And, we could probably get some cheap parts from an auto-wrecking company.''

"Really?" Slowly Patsy turned to face him. "You would do that for me?''

Justin pulled his lips between his teeth and looked at the ceiling before answering. "Sure.''

"Thanks," she breathed and, reaching into the shower, punched his arm in a most buddylike fashion. "You're saving my life again.''

"Anytime," he deadpanned, a small smile tugging at the lips with which she was now so hauntingly familiar.

The days ran one into the other, a blur of activity as the entire camp prepared for Thanksgiving. When Thursday morning finally arrived, cookies and pies and other lovingly—if not expertly—prepared desserts filled one counter of the "mess hall's" crowded kitchen. The other small countertops were lined with two giant overstuffed birds, having been baked to mouthwatering perfection in Holly and Buck's new double oven. Next to these sat piles of mashed potatoes, bowls of cranberry sauce, various breads, vegetables, salads...more food than most of the children had seen in one place in a lifetime.

After thanks were offered—and Holly had each of the children tell what they were grateful for in a touching scene that had reduced Patsy to a sniffling, watery-eyed mess—the meal had been greedily gobbled. The only sounds that could be heard for the better part of an hour that afternoon were the crunching, munching, lip-smacking sounds of hungry, growing children filling their stomachs.

Over the sea of neatly combed heads, Patsy had found Justin's eyes with her own. Slowly a smile spread secretly between them. A smile of understanding and compassion, a smile of bonding between themselves. For if they had nothing else in common, their mutual love for the children was the tie that bound.

When the plates had been cleared and the last crumbs of the pumpkin pie swept away, it was time for the pageant. The kids were delirious with excitement. Clad in paper pilgrim hats and Indian headdress, they performed the story of the first Thanksgiving. Groups trundled in turn to the small stage area for song and poetry recitations.

Patsy sat between her brother and Justin, beaming with emotion and pride as her little boys and girls' dance class stumbled through the routine she'd choreographed for the occasion. Justin, his own eyes suspiciously bright, reached out and clasped her hand in his and squeezed. She squeezed back.

When the festivities had ended, the younger children—supervised by the slowly plodding, but ever smiling, Gayle—had flung off their costumes and rushed outside to the play area for a rousing game of Red Rover. The older children swarmed into the kitchen for a noisy, giggling, mischievous turn at KP duty. As the dishes were being scrubbed and tossed through the air to be miraculously caught by those with towels, Buck and Holly and several of the counselors retired to one of the classrooms for some quiet time and to organize that evening's activities.

Having been left to their own devices, Justin urged Patsy to join him outside to walk off a few of the holiday calories. The giddy laughter of children at play rang out as they stepped into the crisp November air. The weather had finally begun to feel a little like fall.

"I'm so full I could pop," Patsy moaned, and pulled the bulky sweater she'd borrowed from Holly a little more closely around her middle. "At the rate we're going, I'm *never* going to be ready to dance at the reunion."

"How's that going, anyway?" Justin wondered conversationally.

A smile graced his chiseled lips as he fell into step beside Patsy. The sun was peeking from behind some lazily floating clouds, and the trees were losing the last vestiges of their crown of color. It was a beautiful day in a beautiful place. Patsy couldn't remember feeling so content in a long time.

"What, my whipping myself into shape, or whipping the kids into shape?" Her smile was sardonic. They hadn't ventured out jogging since the fateful day of the kiss.

"Both." He peered down at her, clearly interested.

"It's hopeless." Patsy threw up her hands in a plaintive motion, and allowed them to drop to her sides. "I know we've only been working on our routine for less than a week now, but Justin, ohhh," she sighed and shook her head tragically, "those kids all have two left feet. Even the big kids. *Especially* the big kids. Not a dancer in the bunch. With the possible exception of Gayle. But she's *great* with child, and I doubt that we could pull off anything more graceful than elephants on parade, between the two of us."

Justin hooted at that. "The kids are that bad?"

Patsy moaned. "I'm afraid so. And the worst part of the whole deal is, I *promised* them they could perform Saturday night of the reunion with me, and—" she squeezed her eyes tightly shut "—they are really looking forward to it." Biting her lower lip, she stared off at the horizon and grew thoughtful. "I wonder what kind of dance the kids could do, without moving much? Scenes from *The Nutcracker* will be simply out of the question," she murmured. Snapping out of her trance, she shrugged. "Ah, well, I'll figure it out."

"Anytime you want to watch that dance video you were talking about for some ideas, just let me know. I'll make the popcorn."

Patsy smiled at him. "You're on. No butter on the popcorn?"

He rolled his eyes. "Whatever."

"I can't believe the reunion is only four weeks away. We have so much to do. I don't know how we'll get it all done in time."

The children's laughter began to fade as they strolled out behind the paddock and down a trail through the woods that Justin used for horseback riding lessons. As they sauntered along, the sun cast long dappled shadows across the distant wheat fields, signaling the end to another holiday.

"What are you talking about?" Justin queried with a puzzled frown. "Four weeks is plenty of time to get ready for a simple reunion."

"That's just it. It's not simple."

"Why not?"

"Well, first of all, I can't go to this thing in one of the half dozen outfits I shoved into my suitcase, the day I left Big Daddy's. So we need to go shopping. And, you need to get the car running. And, and we need to spend some time rehearsing our roles, and we need to spend some time with Marky and Mikey so that we'll seem more like a, uh, er, family, and we need...to spend...some...time..." She glanced up at Justin, and saw the corners of his lips twitching.

Her eyes narrowed to a glare. "What? What's so funny?"

"You." He shrugged. "Me. I don't know. I guess I just can't believe we are going through with this."

"Believe it." Her voice was glum.

"Hey, don't be so downhearted." He threw a companionable arm around her shoulders. "It will all work out in the end."

Looking at him, his jaw set with determination, his eyes filled with understanding, Patsy could almost believe him. Almost. But not quite. He still hadn't seen the kids dance. Without her realizing it, her arm stole around his middle, and she hooked her fingers through his belt loop as they ambled together through the scenic woods.

"Maybe," she sighed, "you're right. Still, I'd feel a lot better if we…" She felt the heat rush from the pit of her stomach to her cheeks. "You know." She didn't want to seem pushy, especially in light of the fact that he didn't want this whole thing to get too personal. "If we…" She punched him in a buddy fashion with her free arm. "If we spent some more time together, getting ready. At the very least, we need to do some shopping."

Justin pulled a beleaguered face, which Patsy suspected was more teasing than tolerant. "Okay. Let's go—" he shuddered "—shopping."

"How about tomorrow? We have the day off."

"The day after Thanksgiving? Are you nuts? That's the busiest shopping day of the year."

Patsy whapped him with another buddy-type punch in the arm. "Oh, c'mon. It'll be fun."

Chapter Seven

"**P**atsy, I'm not going back to the mall again today, and that's final." Folding his arms over his chest, Justin narrowed his eyes, warning her from across the booth they shared in the tiny luncheonette.

"But we haven't bought anything yet," she argued, pulling a paper menu out of the holder and tossing it across the table at him.

"So?" Justin frowned. Did women always have to purchase something? Was a shopping trip incomplete if a dollar or two was not saved at a sale rack? Lifting his furrowed brow, he wondered over what made the feminine mind tick.

Rolling her menu into a tube, Patsy slanted her gaze at him. "So...what are we going to wear to the formal reunion party? We certainly can't wear matching Miracle House Ranch sweat suits."

"Why not?" He grinned.

Patsy snorted. "You're hopeless."

With a grunt, Justin picked up the paper menu and unfurled it in front of his face.

Today, the first Friday after Thanksgiving, was notoriously the busiest shopping day of the year. And, much to Justin's eternal chagrin, he'd been commandeered into spending his day off hunting for—he scrunched his face into a tortured wad for a moment, then blinked—formal reunion garb. *Yeesh.* Formal reunion garb that he would wear while posing as Dr. Oscar Madison, plastic surgeon and, most likely, rubbing elbows with the up-and-coming Bitsy Hart and her self-important crowd.

Aw geez.

Dropping the menu, Justin rubbed his weary eyes, and wondered how he'd allowed himself to be talked into this debacle. Slowly lifting his lids, he focused on Patsy. The answer sat across from him.

Patsy Brubaker.

Mrs. Oscar Madison, Ph.D., famous European dancer, former space shuttle pilot...his wife. At least for the reunion. Nobody, but nobody—other than the perky little minx that fidgeted huffily in her seat at the other side of the table—ever could have talked him into this mess. Nobody. Not even Darlene, after they'd seriously discussed marriage.

Patsy smacked the tabletop with her rolled up paper menu. "Fine," she grumbled. "You can wear a cummerbund and a bow tie with your disgusting, horsey smelling, manure spattered blue jeans to the alumni party. See if I care. I'll simply—" she flapped her hands in exasperation "—tell everyone that you just came from a really tricky nose job, and didn't have time to change."

Justin chuckled at her feisty expression. He was really beginning to enjoy their verbal sparring. Life was so much less dull when Patsy was around. Until he'd been drafted into this harebrained charade they were planning, he'd never spent more than a moment here and there in her company, and hadn't realized how her zest for living could spice up even the most mundane activities. Even spending the morning slogging through men's stores hadn't been all *that* terrible.

Especially enjoyable were the moments when she'd grab him and order him to stand close while she held various items of clothing up to his body, checking for size and color and heaven only knew what. She smelled all flowery and girlish and this particular olfactory treat was something he rarely experienced out in the horse barn with the other Miracle House ranch hands.

Several times already that day, as she'd stuffed him into various shirts and tugged at his waistband, he'd had the wild, and decidedly stupid, urge to slip his arms around her waist and press himself into the generous curves of her petite body. To bury his face in her neck and inhale the scent that made Patsy so uniquely feminine. To tilt her mouth up to his and taste those plum-colored lips, so ripe for kissing.

But then she'd spot some bargain or another across the room and skip off, leaving him to wonder what had become of his sanity.

He had to constantly remind himself that she was Buck's younger sister. No doubt Buck would not be too happy with him if he knew what had been going through his mind lately. Buck was extremely protective of Patsy.

All the Brubaker brothers were.

Justin tugged at the collar of his shirt. *Good grief.* Why was he obsessing on kissing his future partner's sister this way? Was he trying to ruin his chances at partnership? His career? His life? Grimacing, he plunged a shaky hand through his hair.

Man. He'd been too long outside of a meaningful relationship. He'd better start thinking about asking somebody out. Anybody. Anybody but Patsy Brubaker.

Squirming in his chair, Justin dropped his menu and peered at her.

"What are you going to have?" he asked, attempting to derail his train of thought.

"I don't know," she mused, as she unrolled and scanned her menu. "Something light. A side salad and a glass of water, I guess."

Justin tilted his menu down and frowned at her. "Ah, come on. Get some real food. My treat." They hadn't eaten since breakfast, which, according to his watch, was now hours ago. He was starving.

He'd deliberately chosen the small, rather shabby-looking luncheonette across the street from the shopping center in order to save money. The sign in the window had boasted a $4.99 Special, and since Justin had never been one to go into debt—preferring to pay cash for everything from a suit of clothing to lunch—he'd figured what the heck? Being the volume eater that he was, he could fill his belly for under five dollars. Shoot, the special couldn't be any worse than the messes Buck threw between two slices of bread on a late work night.

Closing her menu, Patsy set it aside and propped her heart-shaped chin in the palm of her hand and smiled ruefully at Justin. "No, I think a salad will be more than enough. I still have five pounds to go."

"Five pounds?" Justin tossed his menu on top of hers and looked at her incredulously. "That's nothing. What possible difference can five pounds make?"

"Well." Patsy shrugged and pulled her lower lip between her teeth. She thought for a moment. "Being five pounds overweight is like carrying around a couple of two and a half pound bags of potatoes in each thigh."

Justin hooted. He wasn't sure if it was her completely earnest expression, or the mental picture her words evoked. How ridiculous. Her thighs were perfect. He knew. He'd held them in his hands all the way across Hidden Valley and out to the ranch last Sunday morning.

"Look, nobody at the reunion is going to care if you lose five pounds or not. Especially when you don't need to."

"But I *do!* You *know* that even after three kids, Bitsy is going to look like something out of an underwear catalog."

Justin's eyes followed her movements as she crossed her arms defiantly under her breasts. *Heaven help me,* he silently pleaded and allowed his head to drop back against the high leather back of the booth. "So who cares what Bitsy is wearing or what Bitsy looks like? What difference does it make?"

"You still don't get it, do you?" she sighed. Finally the waiter arrived to take their order and Patsy fairly beamed with relief.

"No," Justin muttered. "I don't get it." He'd had this argument before with Darlene. And it bored him.

He ordered the special, hoping to tempt her into eating, when the time came. Patsy ordered a small green salad, dressing on the side and a glass of water. The special turned out to be double bacon cheeseburger, dripping with grease and cholesterol and a giant side of fries. It looked and smelled divine. And, as he dug in, he decided it was.

They ate in silence for a while, both deciding it was safer to ignore the subject of her diet. He caught Patsy hungrily eyeing his fries, but she was far too stubborn to yield to temptation.

Polishing off the last of his burger, Justin leaned back and patted his stomach. "That's better," he said with a grin.

"Mmm," Patsy agreed, as she viciously chased her last crouton around her plate with a fork. "So," she said with a smile. Dropping her fork with a clatter on her empty plate, she glanced at her watch. "We'd better get a move on, if we're going to get everything we need for all the various functions Bitsy has planned. Are you ready to go? I want to check out a couple of sale racks I saw on the way over here.''

"No."

"No?"

"I told you, I'm not going back to the mall."

"But," Patsy protested, her expression suddenly crestfallen, "what will we wear to the formal functions?"

"Not some overpriced getup from some overpriced store at the overpriced mall, that's for sure," he informed her, somewhat grumpily. He'd gotten a load of the tags on a couple of the outfits she'd thrust under his chin.

Neither of them could afford such exorbitant prices. Not when she was saving for a new car, and he for his new house. Since he'd purchased the property next to Buck and Holly, he'd been reviewing floor plans. As soon as he was able, he would begin the building process. Someday very soon, he and Buck would begin their partnership and begin their fund-raising efforts in earnest. Then the salaries for everyone involved would loosen up quite a bit.

For now, though, he'd just have to tighten the old belt a notch or two. He didn't want to go into debt any sooner than necessary on the house, and that included wasting money on fancy clothes to impress the likes of Bitsy Hart. Patsy had yet to get a tight grip around the idea of a budget.

Justin smiled at her bemused expression. He had to admit, living next door to Patsy this last week had been enlightening. And, a lot of fun. Much more fun than was prudent, he was sure. Having her living in his own backyard had given him the opportunity to get to know Patsy on a more intimate level.

Something about Patsy had him eager to bounce out of bed in the morning and greet the day. To race her to the coffeepot in the main office. To wrestle her away from the ancient copy machine when he needed it. To sit on her desk and drive her nuts while she tried to work. To simply spend time in her presence.

Justin knew he should be a lot more worried about becoming involved with her, but somehow he was just having too doggone much fun. Ah, well. Everything would work out in the end, he knew. No amount of worry would change a thing. So, for now, he would just enjoy the exhilarating company of Buck's sister.

Soon enough the reunion would be over, and he would have to go back to the single life. Back to being Marky and Mikey's sole guardian until their aunt regrouped and came back. And, back to the somewhat daunting task of finding a woman who suited his lifestyle and was patient enough to wait for his particular ship to come in.

He sighed.

The idea exhausted him.

Justin glanced at Patsy and wondered briefly what she wanted in a man. Ah, well, never mind.

It wasn't anyone like him, if her similarity to Darlene was anything to go by.

"Are you going to eat those?" Patsy pointed nonchalantly at a small pile of fries he had yet to attack.

Justin slid his plate across the table with a grin. "No, but be careful, now, there is probably a calorie or something lurking in there."

"Oh, be quiet," she mumbled around a satisfying mouthful, the corners of her mouth stealing into a tiny, playful smile.

Justin didn't know if Patsy had noticed the subtle changes that seemed to take place with startling regularity in their relationship or not, but he was sure, on more than one occasion, he'd caught her staring at him.

It was almost as if she were trying to figure out what to do with their newfound friendship.

He studied Patsy's hauntingly beautiful face for a moment. The face that shadowed his dreams every night. An inch at a time, she was becoming part of his nights. His days.

His heart.

He shook his head to clear it. Dammit, he had to stop thinking about her that way. It was bad for his business relationship with Buck, and that was bad for the future of the ranch. It was definitely bad for his blood pressure.

Pulling his wallet out of his rear pocket, he tossed several bills on top of the check, and his mouth quirked with exasperation as he looked at Patsy.

"What now?" she wondered, suspicion lurking in the bright blue depths of her eyes.

"Come on," he urged, sliding out of the booth and holding his hand out to her. "I have an idea."

Shrugging in resignation, she grasped his hand, and followed him to the door.

Patsy took a deep breath of air as she hurried down the sidewalk in Justin's wake. The "day-after-Thanksgiving" crowds jostled her to and fro, making it difficult to keep up with his lankier stride. She had no idea where he was taking her, and decided that allowing herself to be tugged would certainly be easier than arguing with him. Especially when he made up his mind about something.

She was beginning to discover, the man could be very determined.

As she scurried after him, their linked hands her only lifeline to him in the sea of humanity on the sidewalk, her thoughts wandered back to the evening that he'd forced her to evacuate the war zone that she had called home. A small smile played at her lips. Yes, he was a determined one. Nearly as determined as her father, Big Daddy Brubaker. And, that was saying something.

Filling her lungs with the crisp fall air, she exhaled in hopes of blowing away the feelings of desire she felt growing toward her brother's employee. But it wasn't easy. Especially with his large palm enveloping her smaller hand, sending chills and thrills through her body. Good heavens. Back at the men's store at the mall that morning, she'd nearly made a fool of herself and given in to the absurd impulse to lean into Justin's hard, muscular body and lift her mouth to his for another heart-stopping kiss.

Taboo. She knew.

She exhaled heavily.

Justin didn't want a personal relationship. He'd made that perfectly clear.

Why did she always want the things she couldn't have? she wondered morosely. A car that ran. A bullet-proof apartment. A dance career, at the ripe old age of twenty eight. What had possessed her to want a career in dance in the first place? It was backbreaking, spirit-breaking work. Not to mention the fact that it made any kind of family life impossible.

Yes, she always wanted what she couldn't have.

And Justin had made it perfectly clear that she couldn't have him. Many a night this last week, she'd lain awake and burned with embarrassment over how she'd practically dragged him on top of her for a kiss last Sunday morning. How humiliating. Whatever had possessed her?

Possibly the gallant gestures he'd made rescuing her all over the place. Possibly the deep green eyes, fringed by impossibly thick brown lashes. Or, possibly, the warm muscles that had fairly rippled beneath her touch. Whatever the reason, she'd made a complete fool of herself that morning. Luckily Justin was not the type to rub her nose in her mistake.

Quite the opposite, actually. In fact, since Sunday morning, he'd been the perfect gentleman, treating her like the sister he'd never had. It was driving her bonkers.

They'd made a pact, and however difficult, she intended to keep her end of the bargain. Unfortunately, that morning as they shopped the men's stores, it had been all she could do to honor their agreement.

His Roman statue-type, perfectly chiseled lips had hovered so alluringly over hers as she reached around his waist, moving and smoothing different articles of clothing into place over his rock-solid body. His sleepy eyes, the little creases at the corners of his perfectly sculpted mouth, the tiny cleft in his chin, the arrogant lift to his brow...

Land sakes. At one point she'd had to pretend to suddenly discover an irresistible bargain across the room, and then literally bolt out of the range of his magnetic appeal, before she'd given in to the urge to stand on tiptoe and plant a not so chaste kiss on that handsome mouth of his.

Patsy knew she had better stand back and get a grip. If she was going to survive the aftermath of her class reunion posing as Justin's wife with her emotions in one piece, she was going to have to gird herself against his potent attraction. Getting too carried away with this fantasy would certainly cause nothing but heartache. Besides, she'd given in to far too many crazy impulses lately. Emotional involvement with her brother's devastating friend was one headache that none of them needed.

She would force herself to stop thinking such ludicrous thoughts about Justin and concentrate on getting through the reunion. That would certainly require enough energy to keep her out of trouble.

She hoped.

Stopping in the middle of the sidewalk, Justin reached behind his back and pulled her to his side. He grabbed her by the shoulders and propelled her toward the door of a large building that Patsy could only assume had once been a supermarket.

However—if the window display containing a nude mannequin, his backward toupee falling rakishly over his eyes as he jauntily road a bicycle with two flat tires was any indication—this establishment no longer sold groceries. Her eyes caught the badly hand-lettered sign that was tacked above the door.

One Man's Garbage, Thrift Shop, it read.

"What's this?" she asked skeptically. Her smile was uncertain as they entered the musty smelling store that was literally packed with discarded odds and ends. "One Man's Garbage? The name sure fits," she murmured, staring at the rack of cracked and chipped dishes that stood by the front door.

Surely Justin didn't expect them to shop for their reunion clothes here.

"I thought we could shop for our reunion clothes here." Clasping his hands, he rubbed them together, his gaze wandering eagerly around the store. "You know what they say. One man's garbage is another man's treasure. Pretty neat, huh?"

Her jaw fell slack as she stared up at him. "Pretty and neat are not two words that come to my mind," Patsy said, allowing her eyes to follow his. A tattered sign that hung from the ceiling by a wire hanger said all tags marked with pink dots were fifty percent off. He had to be kidding. "You have to be kidding." Smiling quizzically, she moved to stand in the path of his sweeping, glassy-eyed gaze.

"No." He shook his head, a small frown marring his brow as he regarded her.

"No?" she repeated, her smile fading.

"No. When I was a kid, I, and a bunch of my friends, would shop here for clothes and stuff, when we had extra money. Which was rare."

As if on cue, a swarm of grungy looking teens pushed through the front door and began to enthusiastically paw through the merchandise.

"See," Justin whispered, pointing at their multicolored, multilength, multibeaded-tied-roped-shaved heads of hair. "These kids are on fashion's cutting edge, and they shop here."

Nodding slowly, Patsy watched one happy camper lift the toupee off the naked mannequin in the window and add it to his own crazily coiffed hair. "But, Justin, I'm not sixteen anymore. And besides, I don't think doctors' wives wear grunge. I can't show up at the formal reunion functions looking like *that!*" she hissed, pointing to one particularly ratty teen.

"Who says you have to look like that?" he asked, taking her hand and leading her through the store toward the back. "Give me some credit, will ya? They have a few nice things here."

"A few…nice…things," she repeated dully, sure that he had to be mistaken. Sure that she would hate every moth-eaten moment of this whole ridiculous episode. Bitsy had most likely found her reunion outfit in a Parisian boutique, and here *she* was, browsing through the racks at One Man's Garbage.

Ohh, she groaned inwardly, vowing never to falsify—even as a joke—answers on a document again.

True to his word, Justin led her to a corner that contained several racks stuffed with discarded prom dresses, rejected bridesmaids' dresses, and dresses that looked as if they may have at one time been used in a Las Vegas-type all-girl review.

"Look, Patsy," he said enthusiastically, "all kinds of fancy stuff that has barely been worn." Pulling out several things that drew his attention, he held them up. "This one would go great with your eyes."

"I don't know..." she protested, lifting her gaze from the teeny, blue sequined, strapless gown he held out to her.

Averting her eyes, she touched her tongue to her lower lip. *He'd noticed her eye color?* Something warm and tingly radiated down her arms. A feeling of buoyancy enveloped her as she watched him check the price tags.

He was so funny and thoughtful. She couldn't believe how unfair she'd been in some of her earlier assumptions about Justin. He was really very nice. And he was so darned cute. Boyish charm practically oozed from every perfectly formed pore. How could Darlene have let him get away?

Closing her eyes, Patsy shook her head, hating herself for falling victim to his spell again and trying to forestall the impulse she felt taking over her rational mind. The impulse to throw herself heart first into the moment and revel in his exciting company, and the adventure that they would face together in a matter of weeks.

Patsy's rational mind warned her not to get too hooked on Justin. She wasn't his type. He could never be happy with her. Nevertheless, unable to control the direction of her eyes, she continued to stare up at him in a doe-eyed fashion that was reminiscent of Nancy Reagan watching her husband give a State of the Union Address.

"This one has a pink dot. That means fifty percent off," Justin exclaimed, examining the blue sequined cocktail gown. "And there's nothing wrong with it. Unless you count a couple of these sparkly things that fell off back here by the zipper. Who would ever notice that? Let's see," he murmured, calculating the savings with his businessman's mind, "the thrift shop wanted forty, but it's got a pink dot. It's never been worn, because the original tag is inside. Man!" Darting Patsy a quick, incredulous look, he studied the tag. "It was originally five hundred and seventy-five dollars."

Holding it up to her curves, Justin eyed her appreciatively. He allowed his hands to linger at her hips and under her arms a little longer than necessary as he copied the routine she'd done on him earlier, and smoothed the dress over her body.

"Hmm, well I'll bet you money that it only cost that much because it's got a designer label." He snorted with male indignation. "If you wanted it, you could get it for twenty bucks."

Patsy's eyes suddenly refocused from their glazed adoration and zeroed in on the designer label and gasped. She didn't even have one of *these* in her closet at Big Daddy's house.

"*What?* Let me see that," she squealed in disbelief. Snatching the dress from Justin's hands, she quickly disappeared behind the dusty curtain that unsuccessfully attempted to shield the dressing room. "I'll just be a minute," she sang, her voice breathy from the heady mixture of the virile man that had smiled so indulgently at her just now, and the gold mine she held in her hand. Justin was right. Who cared if it was missing a sequin or two at the back? Nobody would ever notice that.

"Take your time," Justin called back and lowered himself into a rickety chair just outside the cluttered fitting area. He crossed his ankles out in front of him and settled in to wait for Patsy to emerge, curves overflowing, in the sparkly scrap that at one time had cost almost three times more than her car.

Chapter Eight

It had been worth the wait.

Man, Justin thought, as he popped a bag of popcorn into the microwave later that evening, *had it ever been worth the wait.*

Emerging from the dilapidated dressing room, shimmering like some kind of blue-green goddess from an old-time Hollywood epic, Patsy had well and truly taken his breath away. Her fair skin had glowed in silky, smooth contrast to the thousands of sparkling lights that made up the dress, and her iridescent eyes reflected echoes of the midnight sky. Hills and valleys, and curves and planes all came together to form a sight that he wouldn't soon forget. It had been all he could do to keep his hands locked in his lap as he'd sat staring at her and groping for the proper words to express his sense of awe.

Patsy mistook his silence as disapproval, and it had taken some time to convince her that she didn't look fat. Luckily he'd managed to assure her that the dress would do, and after locating a pretty decent used tux for himself, they'd gathered their booty and headed home.

Since it was Friday, they'd agreed it was the perfect time to spend the evening together studying the dance video she'd told him about. So, after a busy afternoon and evening, Patsy had headed to the video store while he'd read a nighttime story to Marky and Mikey and then tucked them—and the rest of the five- to eight-year-old boys—into bed.

The light clumping sound of feet treading up the stairs at his front door pulled him from his blue sequined trance.

"Hi." Justin pulled his head up from where he'd been peering into the microwave. "Any luck?" The popcorn was just beginning to pop, and already smelled wonderful.

Patsy strolled across the room sniffing the air as she went. "Yep." She held up two dance videos and tossed them on the kitchen table. "These are all the rage. You'll see why." She pointed to the cover. "This guy is amazing. Oh, and I checked the mail. Bitsy sent me copies of all the advertising she's done on our upcoming dance performance for the reunion." Her expression was suddenly filled with woe as she held up the thick envelope. "I'm only surprised she didn't alert *Time* magazine."

Tucking his chin into his shoulder, Justin peered behind him at the pile of mail in her hand and smiled sympathetically. The microwave beeped three times, signaling that cooking was complete. He removed the bag of popcorn from the microwave, and rummaged through the cupboards until he located a bowl. Then, he ripped open the bag, dumped the popcorn into the bowl and liberally sprinkled it with salt.

"That bad, huh?" he asked as he worked.

"Yep," Patsy groaned on a weary puff of breath. "That bad. The way she's talking me up to the general public, there will be more 'fans' in the audience than classmates." For a moment she stared forlornly at the various press releases, then tossed them on top of the videos.

"Have some popcorn," Justin encouraged, in order to take her mind off matters.

"This," she said pointedly, lifting a handful to her mouth, "is not the low-fat kind."

Justin scowled into the bowl in mock surprise. "It's not?" came his indignant query. Stifling a grin, he stared at her, wide-eyed. He hated the fat-free popcorn. Tasted like cardboard. Give him the hot, salty, fluffy, buttery stuff any day.

She shrugged. "No biggie. It's good."

Pretending remorse, he exhaled heavily. "I guess we'll have to make do."

"Yep," Patsy agreed, stuffing another handful into her mouth. "It's better than nothing." Grinning, she pulled her gaze into a collision course with his. "Uh, are you ready?" She gestured at the videos. "To, uh, get started?"

Tossing a piece of popcorn up into the air and catching it with his mouth, Justin nodded. "Yep." His eyes never lost contact with hers.

Patsy shivered. With anticipation, or chill, she couldn't be sure. Something had changed irrevocably between them since that Sunday morning, when he'd so gallantly rescued her from her fitness folly.

There must be something about riding through town on a man's back that made a woman feel…somehow closer, so much sooner than the regular getting-to-know-you methods, Patsy mused as she stared at him. Perhaps that's what had driven her to leave her arms wrapped so tightly around his neck after he'd laid her on the couch that morning.

The air fairly crackled with frustration, as they stood across the room, staring at each other just now. Patsy felt a longing in the quiet corners of her heart that she hadn't ever experienced before with any other man. Not with Henri, her European beau. Not with any of the guys she dated back in high school. Not with anybody.

Involuntarily she brought her palm to her chest, and felt the fluttering beneath her breast. Lodged in her heart, along with this yearning, was a fear that she was letting herself in for a world of hurt. After all, she and Justin had no real future together, other than the class reunion.

Anyone could see that.

"It's very good," she breathed, attempting to snap herself out of this reverie.

"Pardon?"

"The popcorn." She pointed. "It's good."

"Oh. Great. There's plenty."

He continued to stare at her in a most unnerving fashion, till Patsy, unable to take the pressure, averted her gaze. Pulling the dance videos off the kitchen table, she held them up. "I'm ready if you are." She pretended great fascination with the box covers.

"Let's do it." He grinned and grabbed the bowl of popcorn.

"Right," she breathed, and followed him to the family room.

While Patsy plugged the first video into the VCR, Justin lowered the lights and tossed a pile of pillows to the floor in front of the couch.

"I thought we should be comfortable for this study session," Justin told her as he unceremoniously dropped to the floor and sprawled lazily out, making himself at home among the pillows. Looking askance at her with a smile, he patted the spot by his side in invitation. "Come on. Have a seat. I always learn better when I'm comfortable."

The dance video flickered to life on the television screen in his darkened living room, and Patsy stood, vacillating. Should she sit on the couch and keep her distance, her dignity and their pact intact? Or, should she sit on the floor by Justin and chance making an idiot out of herself by giving in to her nutty penchant of late to put some kind of move on him?

She chose idiot.

Moving through the shadows to his side, she dropped to her knees and eased herself into the little sitting area he fashioned from the cushions. Yes, she thought, her breathing shallow as she felt the nearness of his warm body, smelled the scent of his fabric softener, saw the outline of his handsome features. Yes, she was asking for trouble.

But, it was too late to suddenly stand up and move to the other side of the room, wasn't it? That would seem rude. And she didn't want to seem rude. Not after the man had been such an angel of mercy in so many ways. No, that wouldn't do at all.

Patsy swallowed and groped for something conversational to take her mind off his thigh, as it rested lightly against hers.

"This is the dance troupe that I'm pretty sure I wrote on my questionnaire that I had, uh, performed with—" she winced as the lead dancer, his feet jack-hammering a frantic staccato on the dance floor, sailed across the stage "—when I was in Europe," she said by way of explanation. "I'm pretty sure I didn't erase that stuff, because I thought I was throwing the questionnaire away. So, unfortunately, Bitsy thinks I used to dance with these guys."

As he watched the screen in wonder, Justin's jaw dropped. "You told Bitsy that you could do *that?*" Angling his head, he stared at her aghast. "You can't even jog a mile! How the hell are you going to pull *that* off? How the hell are the *kids* going to pull that off?"

Eyes wide with wonder, he pointed at the madly tapping man on the screen as he literally flew through the torturous routine. Then, as this whirling dervish pranced and leapt hither and yon around the stage, his troupe—dancing like the pistons on a smoothly running engine—tapped up behind him in a single line, smiling as easily as if this frenzied footwork were the way they normally walked. Like a human metronome on speed, they hotfooted it through one of the most amazing dances either of them had ever seen.

Dragging his eyes from the screen, Justin focused on Patsy.

"You have *got* to be kidding."

"We still have four weeks," she snapped, knowing he was right. Squinting with determination, she jutted her jaw at the screen. "We'll all just have to get into…shape. Maybe I should take the kids jogging," she mused aloud.

"Honey, Arnold Schwarzenegger is in pretty good shape, but I doubt that *he* could do this."

Patsy sagged.

Together, their eyes strayed back to the screen. The lead dancer, his feet a mere blur, his shirt unbuttoned to the waist, a boyish smile pasted to his face, continued to dazzle with frantic gyrations and undulations that were tiring just to watch.

This guy made Fred Astaire look lazy.

"*Ohhhh,* Justin," she moaned and flopped back onto the pillows beside him. Closing her eyes, she flung her hands over her face and moaned again. Loudly. "*Ohhhh!* You're right. I'll be lucky if the kids don't trip and fall simply getting onto the stage, let alone dancing like this…this…*tornado!*" Spreading her fingers she peered through the cracks at his face and whispered miserably. "What are we going to do?"

"Have some popcorn?" he offered helpfully, holding the bowl out to her.

"No, thank you."

"Now, darling," he teased, using the pet name he used to torture her with since she'd commandeered him into posing as her husband. "Darling, you have to keep up your strength, if you are going to dance like these guys.'' Justin angled his head at the TV.

Patsy stared at him slack-jawed, then, unable to help herself, dissolved into a fit of giggles at the thought of the mess in which she found herself. *"Ohhh,"* she cried, flopping back on the pillows, ''I'm toast.'' Weakly, she waved his popcorn-filled hand away from her face.

''Now, darling, don't lose hope. Maybe there is some kind of Evelyn Wood speed dancing course you can take!''

Patsy hooted and tossed a pillow at his head.

Justin simply ignored her missile and loaded his hand with buttery popcorn. ''Well, at any rate, we can't have you fainting from hunger in the middle of your performance. You need sustenance for the kind of labor intensive workout you are planning. Here, darling,'' he continued to tease, with a rather wicked gleam in his eye, ''please, allow me to feed you. Come on, my little liebchen. Eat!'' he playfully commanded, tossing popcorn at her chin and mouth. ''You need your strength.''

"Auggh!" Patsy giggled, pushing at his hands as he tried to cram bits of popcorn between her lips.

''You're not cooperating, darling,'' Justin teased and grabbed her flailing wrists. ''Stick with me,'' he grunted, laughing himself now. ''I'll have you dancing like a wild woman in no time!''

"Auggh!" Patsy shrieked again, dissolving with him in unrestrained laughter. Their bellies shook all the harder as they glanced up to see the European dance team kick it into high gear and rocket across the stage. Clutching each other, they gasped and howled till the tears streamed down their cheeks.

''If I get you a billowy white shirt and some tight black pants, would you dance with me?'' she squeaked, rocking back and forth on her bed of pillows.

''Of course, darling,'' Justin quipped, ''but I think you

just want to see me in tight pants." He leered wolfishly through the darkness at her, still laughing.

"Mmm. You may be right, Dr. Oscar," she said and wiped her eyes with the back of her hand.

Sprawling on his side, Justin hauled Patsy up against him and nestled the bowl of popcorn between their bodies. Then, leaning forward in the dim light of the flickering TV screen, he sobered and traced her lips with a piece of popcorn.

"Oh, no, no, no. I shouldn't," she demurred, not sure exactly what it was that she shouldn't do, but knowing that in any event, she…shouldn't.

"Come on," he tempted. "Live a little."

Unconsciously she parted her lips and allowed him to push the popcorn inside her mouth. He did so with slow, deliberate movements, then licked the salt from his fingers. Patsy tried to swallow past the lump of excitement that had suddenly taken up residence in her throat.

Oh boy, oh boy, *oh boy*. Her heart seemed to be pounding out the words. *Ohboyohboyohboy*. Patsy's pulse raced faster than the lead dancer's feet.

Live a little, Justin had advised. Famous last words. Whenever she'd given in to such impulses in the past, she'd lived to regret it. She'd chosen dance as a career goal without realizing all it truly entailed. No, Patsy wasn't about to travel down another pointless life trail. She simply had to get over this infatuation with Justin. Sometime soon.

But…maybe not at this exact minute.

"Justin," she murmured breathlessly as he slowly leaned forward and kissed her cheeks, and then, after many delightfully torturous moments, moved to her eyelids, "we're not going to learn anything about…" She sighed, a mere whisper hovering on the shadows. "The, uh, dance program this way."

"Who cares?" he asked, his voice raspy with desire. He

lightly touched his lips to hers and spoke against them. "The kids can learn a few simple steps these guys use, and do them over and over at the reunion. Piece of cake." Impatient to get back to the business of wooing her, he rained a trail of tiny kisses across her jaw and nuzzled the sensitive spot where her neck met her shoulder.

Patsy felt a flash fire ignite and roar down her spine. "Oh, yeah? You think that will work, huh?"

"Sure. We just need to spend some time practicing," he said, then smiled. "Practice makes perfect, you know."

Patsy's eyes warred with his for a moment before she whispered, "Is that what we're doing here?"

"Yeah," he groaned as he pushed her on her back and brought his lips to rest lightly against hers. "Just practicing."

It was the sound of Buck's voice that finally penetrated their passion-fogged minds and had them springing apart as if they were a couple of kids caught with their hands in the cookie jar.

"Hey, Justin," Buck called and knocked on the screen door of the trailer. Hearing no response, he pulled open the door and let himself and Holly in. "Hey, buddy," he called into the gloaming, feeling his way in the dark.

"Shh, honey," Holly admonished. "What if he fell asleep in front of the TV?"

"Well, we'll wake him up," Buck said, lumbering into the family room, searching for the light switch. "Justin?" As he snapped on the overhead light, his and Holly's surprised and amazed gazes swung to the guilty, disheveled couple that blinked up at him from a bed of pillows in the middle of the floor.

"Patsy?" Buck stared aghast at his sister as she straightened her hair and rumpled clothing and tried unsuccessfully to don a mask of poise. Of cool sophistication.

The last time Buck Brubaker had paid any real attention, his sister and Justin were barely on speaking terms, let alone spending time cuddled together in front of the now snowy TV. A slow grin brought the famous family dimples out of hiding. His look of shock tinged with a bit of admiration—as he gawked at his sister—seemed to say he was seeing her in a whole new light. A light that spoke of her surprising maturity in her choice of boyfriends for once.

"Hi, uh, Buck, Holly," Patsy grunted and, stumbling along with Justin, managed to make it to her feet. She and Justin exchanged flustered glances.

Mortified, Holly tried to smooth things over. "Oh, Patsy! Justin! We're so sorry to, er, interrupt. We simply stopped by to drop off this book we borrowed from Justin on the development of the…the…development—" she stared at them, tongue-tied "—the orphaned child. Here…uh, Justin. Thanks so much. For the book. It was good. You, uh," Holly prattled on, dropping the book on the end table nearest the front door, "just go back to…uh, what you were, uh, doing there." She took several steps back, dragging her now broadly grinning husband by the arm. "Come on, honey," she growled through clenched teeth to Buck. "Can't you see? They're *busy*."

"No! No," Patsy hastened to reassure them, grateful for the reprieve. Her mind was reeling. She needed time to sort out what had just happened to her and Justin. Their timing had been wonderful. And horrible. But, perfect nonetheless. She wasn't emotionally, spiritually, or mentally prepared for the kisses they'd just shared, let alone what might have eventually followed if they'd been left to their own devices.

Unable to bring her eyes to Justin's, she fought the raging inferno that flashed to her cheeks and tried to act as normal as possible, given the thoroughly embarrassing circumstances.

"Please. Stay." She gestured behind her to Justin. "We,

uh, we were simply, uh, studying for our, uh…time at the class reunion there…now…as ah, husband and wife…" she stammered as she ran a hand over the curls that Justin had so effectively tangled.

"Gonna be some reunion," Buck drawled.

Justin grinned. "So far, so good." He inclined his head at his buddy and ran a hand over his whisker-shadowed jaw.

Holly looked back and forth between Patsy and Justin, a puzzled expression on her face. "You're really going to go through with this? I thought it was all some sort of practical joke that you decided to abandon."

Justin shrugged. "It's a long story."

Patsy sighed. "A long, long, very long story."

"Well," Buck said with a grin as he tugged his very pregnant wife to the couch and settled her onto his lap. "It's a lucky thing we don't have anything better to do, right, honey?"

Her curiosity obviously getting the better of her desire to mind her own business, Holly nodded enthusiastically.

"Right, honey."

Later that night, after Buck and Holly had laughed themselves silly for the better part of an hour over Patsy's absurd scheme to fulfill Bitsy's reunion plans, they'd headed up the short road to their home, their hoots of hilarity echoing down the hill and fading into the night as they went.

It was nearing midnight, and though neither she, nor Justin, had to work in the morning, Patsy knew it was time to call it a night as well. She needed desperately to go home and spend some time alone thinking about what had happened that evening. His arm wrapped possessively at her waist, Justin walked her the few feet it took to get her to her own front door.

Cricket song filled the air, and the various autumn smells

permeated the night. Burning leaves. Drying hay. Dust from the driveway, and the crisp, clean fragrance of brisk evening air, as the days slipped toward winter. A delicious shiver skipped down Patsy's spine. A shiver of belonging. Of romance. Of…love? Love of what exactly, she wasn't sure she wanted to admit. At least not yet. Not when she was feeling so perfectly divine.

Pausing at the stoop, Patsy turned in Justin's embrace, and looked up at him as he stood silhouetted against the low-slung harvest moon. Her heart rolled over, and she knew that the stars that pierced the velvet black of the vast Texas sky were surely reflected in her gaze.

"Thank you—" she murmured, knowing that these simple words were inadequate to express the feelings she harbored in the secret recesses of her heart "—for you know, practicing with me and everything."

"My pleasure," he whispered. Bowing his head, he rested his nose lightly against hers. "Practicing with you is some of the most fun I've had in years."

"Me, too."

"We should do it again sometime."

Not sure if this was such a smart idea, Patsy threw caution to the wind and leapt at the opportunity. "How about tomorrow night?"

"How about now?" he asked, his husky voice low in the pale light that shimmered from the moon. His lips touched hers for a moment, nipping and grazing, eliciting a gasp of pleasure from deep in her throat.

"I was, uh, talking about rehearsing our roles for the reunion."

"So was I."

"No, I mean rehearsing with Marky and Mikey and the other kids…"

"Patsy?"

"Huh?"

"Shut up and practice."

For many moments they stood, locked in an embrace that suspended time and space. Justin leaned back against the wall of her trailer, spreading his legs slightly for balance. Pulling her into his arms, he cradled her against his body, molding them together until her shadow became one with his in the milky moon-glow. Again, he kissed her until she was rendered almost senseless with longing.

After many minutes had passed, Justin finally tore his mouth from hers and, breathing heavily, rested his chin on the top of her head.

"Good," he sighed raggedly. "Excellent practice session. We're really starting to get the hang of it, don't you agree?" he murmured, his teasing voice low in her ear. "I think that's about as far as we should go in front of your classmates. Any more public displays of affection would be—" he rubbed his nose against hers "—gilding the lily. Not to mention illegal."

"Mmm," Patsy groaned. "Indecent."

"Immoral."

"Shocking."

"Enjoyable."

"Very enjoyable," she whispered into his mouth, as he claimed her lips for one last air-crackling, thunder-and-lightning kiss.

When their pulses had nearly returned to normal, Patsy was finally able to squeak, "Tomorrow night then? Another practice session?"

"Wouldn't miss it for the world," he promised and kissed her hard one last time on the mouth, to seal the deal.

The following evening found Justin living up to his end of the bargain to spend the evening practicing for the reunion with Patsy. Too bad he hadn't realized that this evening would entail trying to mold the irrepressible Marky and Mikey into talented and gifted child prodigies, ready to showcase Patsy's most-likely-to-succeed virtues as the perfect mother.

Sighing heavily, he ran a hand through his hair, and wondered yet again how he'd managed to find himself in this crazy predicament. He'd never have done anything like this for Darlene.

Glancing down at Patsy as she stood in line with him, waiting for their number to come up signaling that their pizza was ready, Justin suddenly had the sinking feeling that he was in trouble, when it came to this woman. Deep trouble. More trouble than he'd ever found himself in any other relationship so far.

Ruefully his eyes swept the restaurant that Marky and Mikey had chosen for first outing as a "family."

Monkey Business was aptly named. The old-fashioned pizza parlor was literally swinging with precocious, sticky-fingered, freckle-faced, screaming little children, running hither and thither until Justin feared his head would cave in. Thank heavens for Patsy. She seemed relatively unfazed by the noise and teeming activity. Probably stemming from a childhood spent with eight rowdy brothers, he guessed.

A large cage toward the rear of the restaurant was filled with small multicolored plastic balls where several dozen children cavorted, jumping and diving like sea otters. Lights flashed, sirens wailed and old silent movies flickered on a screen that dropped from the ceiling every thirty minutes. Against the far wall, an ancient pipe organ sat on a loft up near the ceiling. Its pipes belched squeaky circus music as a clown pounded on the keys.

The only thing missing, in Justin's opinion, was a roller coaster. He ran a hand from his bleary eyes to his jaw as he searched the throngs that milled by for Mikey's rust-colored head.

When Patsy had suggested taking the boys out to pizza

tonight, she must have caught him when his blood sugar was low, because at the time, spending more time with Patsy, no matter the circumstances, had sounded like a great idea. However, as much as he loved Marky and Mikey, they were more than a handful. And, an evening spent corralling these two renegades was definitely not what he'd had in mind when he'd agreed to another "practice session."

His eyes were drawn magnetically back to Patsy's girlish face, which was puckered in consternation as she also scanned the room for Mikey.

He sighed.

Yep. He was in way over his head. His heart slammed into his ribs.

Heaven help him, was he falling for Buck's sister?

"There he is!" Patsy cried, pointing across the room at Mikey as he stood shifting from foot to foot, obviously looking for the easiest way to scale the pipe organ.

Leaning across Patsy, Justin grabbed Marky as he shot by and pulled him back into line where they'd been waiting for close to an hour for their number to come up on the big flashing yellow banana.

"Stay," Justin commanded Mikey, and peered toward the direction that Patsy pointed. *Man,* he thought, cracking his knuckles, *these two were harder to corral than a herd of chickens in a hurricane.*

"I'll get him," he told Patsy. To Marky, he shot a menacing look. "Stay," he barked again.

Marky grinned devilishly.

Patsy clutched the boy's jacket. "I've got him."

"Don't let go." Justin rotated his shoulders and headed out after Mikey, as if he were a prizefighter jumping into the ring.

Nodding, she watched his retreating back move into the teeming mob, and was filled with a swirling array of emotions she couldn't begin to sort out. Admiration was at the top of the list, she decided, as her eyes drank in the picture of the strikingly handsome man who so easily crossed the room and swung the kicking and protesting boy up onto his broad shoulder.

After a brief—and somewhat stern—conversation with the child, Mikey stopped fighting, and it appeared that Justin had won. This round, anyway, Patsy thought with a smile. Lifting a lazy eyebrow in her direction, he grinned and slowly began to make his way back to the line where she stood waiting for their number to come up.

As much as Justin liked to grumble about the boys' lack of discipline, he was really quite wonderful with them, she mused, touched by the happy expression on Mikey's face as he rode on Justin's shoulders. This was only the fourth month they'd been living at the ranch since their aunt—in many ways, still a child herself—had sought help in order to take a much-needed break, but Patsy could see the positive changes happening already. He was very firm with the boys, insisting that they toe the line, and they were beginning to learn that he meant business.

However, his strict demeanor was tempered with a sense of humor that kept the boys giggling, and the three of them had secrets to which Patsy was not privy. She didn't care. She loved watching them put their heads together, whispering, laughing, wrestling.

In fact, earlier that afternoon, after an impromptu lunch of bologna sandwiches—where they rehearsed picnic manners with the boys for the reunion—Justin had stretched out on the lunchroom floor and closed his eyes, only to be attacked by two giggling, wiggling bundles of energy. To hear the shrieks of joyous laughter, one would think that rolling around on top of Justin was better than a trip to Disney World.

Swallowing, Patsy shifted her eyes to the hard, muscular

build that strained against the soft, faded denim fabric of his button-down shirt. Perhaps the twins were on to something.

As Justin waited for an older woman with a walker to move out of his path, Patsy's gaze traveled to his face, and wandered leisurely over the thick, dark hair that curled against his collar, the smooth line of his clean-shaven jaw, the sparkle of his compelling green eyes and the teasing crescents etched deeply at the corners of his full mouth.

Amazingly he seemed unconscious of the fact that he exuded an air of innate sexuality that was hard for any woman to miss. Patsy closed her eyes. Oh, man. She was letting her heart run away with her. Peeking through her lashes, she watched Justin bestow the disabled woman with his devastating smile, and noted the flirtatious response.

Oh, no, she groaned inwardly, blindsided by a sudden insight, *it was happening. Was she falling in love with Justin?* How could that be when she knew that they were completely wrong for each other?

Sighing, she shuffled forward in line, propelling Marky along with her.

"The banana says 348," Justin said, finally arriving at her side with Mikey. "That's us, right?" He pointed up at the flashing yellow sign.

"Uh…" Patsy blinked, trying to resurface from her enlightening, if somewhat disturbing, ruminations.

Tugging at her hand, Marky inspected their receipt. "Yep. That's us," he exclaimed. Excitedly the twins pushed their way up to the counter, and insisted on carrying the pizza to the table.

Justin reached for his back pocket, and moved toward the cashier. "Patsy," he called over the hubbub to where she was still standing in line, "why don't you go find us a table? The boys can carry the pizza, while I pay the bill."

"Okay," she nodded.

Spotting an empty table in the center of the floor, Patsy fought her way through the maze of children and chairs, and dropped gratefully into her seat, still reeling from the sudden impact of her discovery concerning her deepening feelings for Justin. Taking a steadying breath, she decided to push this problem to the back burner and deal with it later. Besides, it was probably nothing, and right now, the boys needed her undivided attention.

Smiling, she watched them stumble toward her, each carrying one end of the large pizza and, grinning from ear to ear. They were great kids. All they'd ever really needed was some attention. Just a little adult, male supervision, from a wonderful guy like Justin, and gracious, she thought in amazement as the boys arrived at the table and dutifully slid the pizza to the center, the little guys had gone from devils to angels.

Maybe they would pass muster at the reunion after all. Relief, and a deep appreciation for Justin suffused her and, sensing his presence, she gazed gratefully up at him, then frowned.

An ominous black thundercloud had formed over his head.

"What's wrong?" she asked, bewildered.

Hands on his hips, he pinned the boys with a murderous glare. "Hand it over."

"Hand what over?" Mikey asked innocently.

"The wallet," Justin growled.

"What wallet?" Marky shrugged.

"*My* wallet. And, then I want the *clown's* wallet. And stop playing dumb. If I have to, I'll turn you both upside down and shake them out."

"Justin?" Patsy asked, looking from him, back to the boys and then back up at him. "What's going on?"

"When I got to the cashier, I discovered that my wallet was missing." His eyes narrowed at the boys. "Imagine my surprise to discover that one of the clowns," he said to Patsy, "you know, the one who pulled quarters out of the boys' ears when we first got here? Well, he was just telling the manager that his wallet was also missing." Justin scowled at the boys. "Out with them."

"That quarter trick was lame," Mikey protested.

"We were just showing him a new trick," Marky explained.

Snapping his fingers impatiently, Justin held out his hand.

After some moaning and groaning and foot shuffling, the wallets in question were finally produced.

"They mugged the *clown?*" Patsy asked incredulously. "Oh, for pity's sake." Unconsciously she stood and moved to Justin's side to present a rather formidable unit of parental censure. He glanced gratefully down at her, obviously appreciating her support. "Boys?" she demanded, her mouth thinning and her no-nonsense tone matching Justin's. "What do you have to say for yourselves?"

"We're sorry?" Marky wondered.

"We won't do it again?" Mikey guessed.

"You got that right." Sighing, Justin rubbed the muscles at the back of his neck. "Let's go." Inclining his head toward the clown who stood leaning morosely at the counter, he grabbed the boys by their collars.

"Go?" Marky asked.

"Where?" Mikey wondered.

"To return the clown's wallet. You have some explaining and apologizing to do."

"Aw, gee," they wailed in unison.

"Don't aw gee, him," Patsy commanded, and pointed dramatically at the forlorn clown. "Get."

As Justin herded the boys away from the table, toward the clown, Patsy felt her heart swell. Someday, Justin Lassiter would make some lucky kids a great dad. And, she sighed raggedly, some lucky woman a great husband.

Chapter Nine

"No, Marky, you can't take your cowboy hat and spurs with you to the reunion."

"But *whyyee?*"

"Because we barely have room to cram everyone and everything in as it is," Patsy said with a harried sigh.

Her stoic smile faded as she stood on her tiny front porch and watched Justin attach the small U-Haul trailer to the hitch he'd installed on the bumper of her station wagon. Slowly her eyes swept her twenty-five-year-old car with the multitude of dents and dings in the quarter panels. It was hard to tell what color the car had originally been beneath the shower of gray primer spots.

Squeezing her eyes tightly shut, she tried not to think of the pathetic picture they would present as they pulled up to the parking lot of the prestigious private school where she'd spent most of her formative years.

All they needed now, she thought, filling her lungs with a hissing sound, was to lash a rocking chair to the roof to complete the look. Expelling a long, beleaguered breath,

Patsy rubbed her throbbing temples and tried to stem the panic that threatened to overtake her.

It was late afternoon, Friday, December 27, and day one of the reunion weekend had finally arrived.

"Marky, honey, go put your suitcase in the travel trailer and then go wash your hands and comb your hair. It's almost time to go."

Raising her voice, she clapped her hands and began to issue orders to the other half dozen preteen kids she'd chosen to accompany her on her fool's errand. Sixteen-year-old Gayle was coming along to assist in keeping the costumes straight, and to help with baby-sitting during the reunion.

"Dexter, help Mikey with his bags. Patrick, remember to bring the satchel with the dance shoes. Charlyn, Patrick, Jana and Megan, you guys ride in the back cubby. Oh, and Dexter, you Gayle, Marky and Mikey are in the back seat. Justin and I will ride in front with the cooler. Everyone, go to the bathroom *before* we leave. We are running late as it is and I don't want to have to pull over for unnecessary pit stops..."

Wringing her hands, she tried to remember the multitude of small details that needed her attention before they left. She glanced at her watch. If they didn't leave in the next fifteen minutes, they would never make it by 7:00 p.m. Tonight was the cocktail-get-reacquainted party. Tomorrow night was...the dance.

Retraining her gaze to Justin, she watched as he supervised the packing of her station wagon. He seemed confident. Good. He'd assured her that the car was in fine running order. It should be. For the last several days she'd been sliding his dinner under the hood to him as he'd grunted and cursed the engine back to life.

For four weeks now, they had *all* worked their heads off, getting ready for her reunion, taking off only enough time to celebrate Christmas. And, when she wasn't working on her act with the kids, she spent an inordinate amount of time perfecting her act with Justin. She wasn't sure exactly how, or when it had happened, but at some point, they seemed to stop fighting their relationship and had instead gone with the flow. And the flow had been thrilling. Wonderful. A dream come true. Justin was irresistible the times he would practice being her husband, and hilarious when he effected his role as Dr. Madison. His plastic surgeon routine was a stitch. More than once she—screaming with laughter—had made him promise not to get too carried away at the reunion. The last thing she needed was to wonder what wild thing or another he'd say to Bitsy and the gang in person.

Yes. They were having a ball. It was almost as if they had mutually decided to enjoy what time they had together while playing the part of a couple, and worry about the future when it got here.

And the kids were having just as much fun.

The kids had been rehearsing like maniacs in an effort to polish their simple routine for the Saturday night show. Costumes had been sewn, glued, pinned and fastened into a pretty credible semblance of an actual dance troupe. Shoes had been polished, hair styled, nails scrubbed. The kids were wild with anticipation, and Patsy had never felt closer to any group of human beings, outside of her wonderful Brubaker family, in her entire life.

For Christmas, Big Daddy, having somehow caught wind of her predicament had sent along new tap shoes—from his holiday home in New England—for the entire team, along with a note that told her how proud he was of the direction she was heading with her life. The kids had gone berserk with delight, tapping crazily around the main hall's new wooden floor. Patsy had watched with tears hovering at the edges of her lashes. Her father never ceased to amaze her. To challenge her. To love her.

Would she ever be half the parent that he was?

Justin's voice, calling to some straggling kids, pulled her back to the present. She took a deep, gulping breath of cool December air and tried to pull herself together. A quick glance at her watch told her that they had to leave in five minutes, if they were going to make it on time.

Five minutes.

She tugged at the collar of her blouse. For some reason, all morning long, Patsy had been feeling as though she couldn't get enough oxygen into her lungs. Nerves, she guessed, as she stood on the front porch and panted in the direction of her hideous car. Yesterday, in a fit of anxiety, she'd tried to talk Justin into renting a luxury car, just for the weekend, but, alas, he'd remained the sensible one.

Flapping a rag he'd been using to wipe off the dashboard, Justin looked up at her as she stood, paralyzed, on her porch.

"You about ready?"

"I guess so."

"You okay?"

"I guess so."

"You still want to go through with this?"

"I guess so."

Tossing the rag into a pail of soapy water, he noted the look of consternation on her face and grinned indulgently.

"I know what you're thinking, honey. This is not the type of car a surgeon would drive. But, hey, I figure nobody's going to see our car, unless you want to pull it into the high school gym during the party," he explained with a shrug of logic, "so we might as well save the dough."

She hated how much sense he was making. The fact that Justin never felt the need for showy displays was one of the things she was beginning to admire most about him.

Considering their respective financial situations, for her to demand a luxury car would make her feel silly and shallow. He was right. At this stage in their lives, they needed to pinch pennies. But, gosh darn it all, anyway. Here she was, heading to her ten-year reunion in a rusted out beater, wearing a secondhand dress—that was missing several sequins in the back—and borrowing somebody else's kids.

Under these circumstances, it was pretty damned hard to feel confident and successful. Most likely to succeed. Ha. Bitsy was going to see through her like a new pair of glasses.

"Come on," Justin called, tossing his keys from hand to hand, "we'd better put the pedal to the metal, if we're going to make it on time today."

"Okay," Patsy sighed and, reaching behind her, locked the front door of her little trailer house, and pulled it closed. Gripping the porch rail, she leaned against it and attempted to gather her flagging nerves. Her stomach gurgled, swirling and whirling, like an overflowing storm drain. "Let's get going then," she said, forcing a note of gaiety into her voice.

After a quick head count, Justin ushered all the kids into their proper seats and buckled them in, making sure everyone had sweaters, drinks, games, munchies and everything they would need to suffer the two-hour trip to Patsy's high school. In no time at all, there was nothing left to do and they were ready to go.

Feeling like a lamb being chauffeured to slaughter, she stood back while Justin wrestled open the passenger door and assisted her into her seat. She stared listlessly out the cracked windshield and waited for him to start the car and back the U-Haul travel trailer down the driveway and out onto the highway to hell.

What in heaven's name had she been thinking? Was she out of her mind? She winced as her steady-handed husband,

Dr. Oscar Madison, plastic surgeon, missed the driveway/ highway juncture and thudded over the ditch.

Ohhh, she moaned to herself, bouncing listlessly against the passenger door. *This was never going to work.*

"Can't we go any faster?" Patsy glanced at her watch for the thousandth time since they'd headed south to Willow Creek. It seemed as if they'd been driving for years. "I thought you said you wanted to, and I'm quoting here, 'put the pedal to the metal.'"

She stared at him, feeling the cottony balls of frustration crowding into her throat, further cutting off her ability to breathe.

Perhaps catching her breath was becoming increasingly difficult because Justin refused to go any faster than thirty-five miles per hour on this godforsaken stretch of highway. For crying out loud, pedestrians could walk faster than they were toddling along.

Or, perhaps it was the constant roughhousing and song-singing that was going on in the back seat. Marky and Mikey were making most of the din right behind her head.

"I'm going as fast as I feel comfortable going, with this engine," Justin explained for the umpteenth time. "I didn't realize what a strain there would be with all these kids and the U-Haul, too. We have plenty of time," he informed her. "What time does this thing start again?"

"Seven o'clock. *Tonight,*" she added, sarcastically.

"Yes, I know, tonight," he retorted. A muscle in his jaw jumped as he glared into the rearview mirror, and proceeded to vent his aggravation on the boys. "Hey! Marky and Mikey! Guys! Knock it off back there, will ya!"

"He was doin' it!"

"Nuh, uh!"

"I don't care who was doin' it. I just don't want to have to pull this car over."

Blinking, Patsy stared at Justin, sure that her father had slipped behind the wheel, when she wasn't looking. Certainly he was driving as slowly as her father liked to drive. Man, she thought, watching the vein throb at the side of his head, he sure had his parental act nailed down. At least that much was authentic about their little pseudofamily. Much to Patsy's relief, the fracas in the back seat died down for a moment.

Unfortunately the car seemed only too happy to pick up where the kids left off.

Bang!

Bang! Bang!

"Justin!" Patsy screamed, "I think someone's shooting at us! Kids, get down!" she directed, waving her arms and urging her little dance troupe to duck below the window.

"Patsy," Justin sighed. Reaching over, he nudged at her to sit up. "Relax, will you? It's just the engine backfiring."

Slowly Patsy sat up and looked sheepishly around. "Sorry," she mumbled, "must be a flashback from my apartment life."

Bang! Bang!

She flinched. Worry crowded between her brows. "Are you sure we're going to make it on time?" she asked.

"What time is it?" Justin barked in irritation.

"Five o'clock. And, stop yelling at me."

"I'm not yelling at you," he yelled.

"Okay. Okay." *Man,* Patsy thought, gasping for air. *He had the husband act nailed down, too.*

"It's two whole hours until seven. See. We have plenty of time."

"Justin, we are still over an hour away from Willow Creek. That's provided we drive the speed limit. Not twenty miles per hour *under* the speed limit. Plus, we still have to check into the Willow Creek Hotel, change our clothes, feed the kids and get them squared away, before we even show up at the high school gymnasium.'' Gripping the armrest of the door, she struggled to breathe. Surely her lungs must have sprung a leak. *Steady, old girl,* she told herself. *Steady.*

The boys began to roughhouse again.

"Okay," Justin said, a muscle twitching in his jaw as he punched the accelerator. *Bang! Bang!* "So…we'll be a few minutes late. No big deal."

"No big deal," she echoed.

"Hey," Justin shouted over his shoulder, as he glared into the rearview mirror. "I mean it! Knock that stuff off!"

Silence suddenly reigned again in the back seat.

"Good," Justin breathed. "Okay now, you guys, listen up." He shot a quick peek at the kids as he signaled and pulled into the passing lane. "When we get to Willow Creek, Patsy and I are going to drop you guys off at the hotel, Marky and Mikey, you two will come with us to the high school auditorium. You two will behave yourselves. Is that understood?"

"Yeah," they answered, grinning devilishly.

"No pocket picking. Is that clear?"

"Yeah."

Oh, good Lord. Rolling down her window, Patsy inhaled as deeply as she was able, given the steel bands of fear that wound around her chest.

"Good," Justin continued. "Tonight, we are going to go to a family party. You will both use the manners we rehearsed all last week. Got that?"

"Yeah."

"You will be very polite to old Mrs. Renfru, and you will not upset her by taking her purse. Do we understand each other?"

"Yeah." The boys nodded.

"Good. And another thing," Justin added. "Call me Dad, will ya?"

Shrugging, the boys nodded again, as if his request was not in the least unusual. "Okay," they agreed.

"You want all of us to call you Dad?" Gayle wanted to know, straining across her burgeoning belly to peer into the front seat.

"Uh, no, sweetheart, just Marky and Mikey," Justin said. "You can call me Justin." To Patsy he muttered, "I'd like to become a father *before* I become a grandfather."

Patsy giggled nervously.

The miles inched by in purgatory for Patsy, as she watched the minutes slowly tick past on her watch, and listened to the kids sing and play. It sounded as if they were tearing the back seat apart.

After what seemed to be an eternity, it was finally six-thirty and they were closing in on Willow Creek. It was official now. They were going to be late. Twisting her fingers together, she wrung her hands in her lap until her knuckles were snow-white. With a sinking feeling, she realized she was a wreck, and the reunion hadn't even started yet.

Luckily they didn't have to dance until tomorrow night.

Get a hold of yourself, Patsy silently commanded, willing her stomach to unclench. Glancing over at the grim set of Justin's jaw, she began to feel guilty. She could tell her tightly strung demeanor was making him miserable. He was doing her a huge favor, coming down to Willow Creek with her, acting as her escort, helping her with the kids and simply being here for her.

"I'm sorry," she whispered, touching his arm, her heart melting at the incredible lengths this sweet man was willing to go, just for her. She didn't know another soul, other than her family, who would ever voluntarily take care of her this way. And, even though he was probably only helping her because she was Buck's sister, she would be eternally grateful.

"Don't be. You're nervous."

"Mmm."

His eyes settled on her. "Stop worrying. We'll be there on time." Reaching across the seat, he pulled her hand into his lap, and rubbed her fingers in a gentle, reassuring caress.

He was doing it to her again, and he didn't even realize it. Causing that warm sensation to spread throughout her stomach, bringing to mind the thrill of his kiss, the fire of his touch. Simply the way he looked at her—with his strong, easygoing self-confidence—infused her with a certain amount of power.

She was amazed to discover that with his sure touch, it became somewhat easier to breathe.

"I know," she whispered and smiled her thanks. Lifting her chin, she stared out the window for a few minutes and filled her lungs with oxygen. They passed a sign that said: Willow Creek, Five Miles. Once again she checked her wrist. Maybe he was right after all. Maybe they would be there on time.

It had become uncommonly quiet in the back seat, and Patsy was beginning to think the kids had all fallen asleep, until she heard one of them begin to moan. It was Marky.

"Daddd?" he groaned.

"What?" Justin asked, glancing over his shoulder.

"I don't feel so good."

"Me eitherrr." This from Mikey.

"You don't feel good?" Justin made the mistake of asking, instead of veering off to the side of the road and whipping open the back door.

As a parent, he still had a thing or two to learn, Patsy thought wryly, as Marky immediately proceeded to lose his lunch all over the back seat. Chaos ensued as the rest of the kids screamed with disgust and laughter. Opening the glove box, she searched it for a napkin or paper towel, but could only locate a road map, several pencils and the vehicle registration. Mikey, not wanting to be left out, joined his brother, retching colorfully.

Bang! Bang! Even the car sounded sick.

Oh, yeah, Patsy thought as Justin—eager to get the boys out of the back seat—pulled a little too far over to the side of the road and suddenly found himself sitting in the ditch. *They were going to be just a little bit late.*

With a death grip on Justin's hand, Patsy hovered outside the double-door entrance to the Willow Creek High School gymnasium. She smoothed her free palm against her blue-green sequined cocktail dress, and hoped that the hastily matched sequins at the back near the zipper weren't all that noticeable. Justin looked simply breathtaking in his secondhand tuxedo.

"Ready?" he murmured, his voice low in her ear as he gave her hand a quick squeeze.

Looking back at him, she tried to smile her confidence. As scared as she was, she couldn't fathom being here without him. Reaching up, she rested her hand against the crisp fabric of his jacket. "Give me a second," she whispered, and leaned against him to steady her ragged nerves. They were already two hours late. What difference would a few seconds make?

"Sure," he said, releasing her hand and running his fingers in a soothing manner over her bare shoulders. "Relax. The boys will be fine."

She glanced down at the twin rust-colored heads. "I know."

After the tow truck had taken them to town, they had dropped the car off at the local garage, checked into the Willow Creek Hotel with all the kids, and then—leaving Gayle in charge of the other kids—forced Marky and Mikey into their reunion suits, and sprinted across the street to the high school gym. As lethargic as the twins had been after their bout with car sickness, their behavior, tonight anyway, was the least of her worries.

No. She was far too busy being worried about everything else.

Even though she'd taken extra care with her hair and makeup, and her new outfit made her feel slightly taller and thinner than usual, she still felt like Cinderella before the fairy godmother's transformation. She couldn't believe it was time for the reunion to begin already. Somehow, she'd managed to convince herself that this moment would never actually arrive. Especially the way Justin had been *putt-putting* along, behind the wheel.

But, here they were.

With a stoic look at Justin, Patsy grasped the handle, gave one of the doors a gentle push and peered warily through the crack. A flood of memories washed over her as she glanced around. The large gymnasium was gaily festooned with all manner of black and orange party decorations, streamers and balloons.

People that she barely recognized milled around, making idle chitchat, laughing casually and partaking of the refreshments. It was obvious that many of these people had kept in touch and were still fast friends.

"Let's go home," Patsy hissed, tugging Justin by the hand. Heavens, she didn't even know these people anymore. Why was she here again? Oh, yes. She was a spineless jellyfish. That's right. Well, that being the case, it was time to slither on out of here.

"But we just got here," Justin protested, standing behind her and peering curiously over her shoulder through the crack in the doors. The boys crowded between them, trying to see what was going on in the gym beyond.

Bitsy had promised that a day care area would be provided for the kids, movies, crafts and games would keep them busy, while the adults renewed their friendships.

"So? If we leave now, no one will ever know that we were here," she whispered up at him, then peeked back through the doors, repelled and fascinated at the same time.

"Just stand here a second and get used to the place," Justin encouraged, clearly unwilling to spend the next five hours driving home, especially since the car still needed a rear wheel alignment and a good hosing out.

"Okay," she agreed, dubiously.

Signs had been painted with black tempera watercolor on endless sheets of orange butcher paper, and read:

Welcome Home Willow Creek Alumni! Happy Ten-Year Reunion!

And much to Patsy's horror:

Willow Creek High School, Home of Patsy Brubaker, Voted Most Likely to Succeed!

Patsy was going to be sick. That did it. She was leaving. Justin could stay, if he wanted, but she was getting the hell out of Dodge.

Unfortunately Bitsy had other ideas.

"Patsy Brubaker? Is that you?" the familiar pert, yet smooth and sophisticated voice from inside the double door queried. Pushing the door all the way open before Patsy could grab Justin and make good her escape, Bitsy reached out and yanked her into the gym.

"Oh, thank heavens you're finally here!" she gushed, her eyes skiffing over Patsy to land with interest on Justin. "We were all beginning to think maybe you'd changed your mind."

"Yes," Patsy said, thinking it lucky that Bitsy had no idea how close to the truth she was. "We made it."

"Good," Bitsy gushed. Her full lips parted to reveal her

perfect pearly whites, as she quickly appraised Patsy's husband. "Hello," she purred, dropping Patsy's hand and reaching for Justin's. "Bitsy Hart. And, you must be Dr. Madison. I feel as if I know you from our many phone conversations." With a dramatic toss of her head, Bitsy sent her long, silky blond hair floating in a cloud around her smooth bare shoulders.

Touching her own hastily pinned chignon, Patsy sucked in her stomach and wished she'd padded her bra.

"Call me Dr. Oscar," Justin commanded in his deep basso profundo. "All my closest friends do."

Patsy nudged him and with murder in her eyes telegraphed him a knock it off message. She was in no mood for fun and games.

However, Justin shrugged and grinned loosely, clearly unable to resist finally getting his chance to play doctor after so many weeks of practice.

"Okay, Dr. Oscar," Bitsy breathed. Tilting her head back and lowering her lids—in that Hollywood starlet fashion that had always worked so well for her—she slanted a coquettish gaze up at Justin.

An unusual stab of jealousy seared through Patsy's brain and she fought the urge to snatch Bitsy bald. Her heart clambering, she lifted her eyes to Justin. And, as if he could read her mind, he moved a fraction closer and pressed his elbow into hers. His lips lifted in a small smile that made her suddenly feel as if she'd been kissed.

"These must be your adorable children," Bitsy surmised, glancing for a moment at the devilishly grinning Flannigan boys as they hovered nearby, gawking up at the interesting woman. Pointing to an area in the corner, Bitsy urged them to run along and make friends with the other kids.

Patsy closed her eyes and crossed her fingers as they scampered off.

"Patsy, you're looking well!" Bitsy chirped. Her eyes raked her over, inspecting her for any changes the years may have brought. "Cute dress," she gushed and pointed at Patsy's outfit. Running her bejeweled fingers over her own skintight, black satin ensemble Bitsy's laugh was lilting, setting her heaving bosom into motion. "I had one just like it once. But, some sequins fell off the back, near the zipper. So—" she waved an airy hand "—I gave it to charity."

"Oh…" Patsy stammered, backing up, and nearly fainting from mortification. *This had been Bitsy's dress?* Thankfully Justin circled her back with his arm, steadying her, and covering the small patch of not quite matching sequins in the process.

She smiled her gratitude at him and murmured, "I'm afraid you're not going to be able to leave my side for the rest of the evening."

"My pleasure," he whispered, pulling her close and with an easy touch, bolstering her flagging confidence. "You look beautiful in that dress."

Patsy found herself smiling in spite of herself.

"Well, come on in and get reacquainted," Bitsy commanded, and gestured to the group of curious classmates that had gathered to stare, "after all, you are the guest of honor. Everyone's been simply *dying* to hear all about your career as a professional dancer."

Several alumni smiled and nodded with interest.

"Oh, no," Patsy demurred. A wave of panic gripped her. Suddenly, all the practicing she'd done with Justin and the kids eluded her. At a complete loss as to what to say to all these ogling faces, she leaned into Justin's rock-solid body. She didn't feel like the guest of honor, she felt like fresh roadkill, being eyed by hungry buzzards. *Oh good heavens!* These folks were going to ask her about a life she'd never lived.

What on earth had possessed her to think she could pull off such a harebrained scheme?

Spots danced before her eyes, and she felt faint until she realized that the spots were coming from the large, mirrored ball that spun lazily overhead as a jazz ensemble played softly in the background. She swung her gaze to Justin's steady green eyes, and felt his strength pass into her quaking body. Once again, his calming, steadying presence was more reassuring to her than he'd ever know.

Linking her slender arm through Patsy's, Bitsy moved between them and twined her fingers chummily with Justin's. Slowly she began to steer them through the throng, pausing now and then and reintroducing Patsy to her curious classmates.

"And, this is her husband, Dr. Oscar, the plastic surgeon," Bitsy announced to a group of her own closest cronies from high school. Smiling in her Cheshire fashion, Bitsy sidled up to Justin and bestowed him with her practiced gaze. To Patsy she said, "You remember the gals from the rally squad? Grace and Brenda and Joyce?"

"Yes." Patsy nodded, her eyes sweeping the gaggle of curious faces that peered at her and drooled over her husband.

"You married a plastic surgeon?" Grace exclaimed, with delight. "How wonderful!" To Justin she said, "Listen, I suppose this must happen all the time, people taking advantage of you to ask medical questions, but since you're practically family, being Patsy's husband and all, I was wondering if you'd have a quick little peekie at this..." Yanking her already plunging neckline even further into the lush danger zone of her feminine attributes, she pointed to a beauty mark on her ample bosom and shot Justin a concerned look. "Doctor, what would you do with this?" she wondered, thrusting her breast up under his face for his inspection.

"Well, I can tell you what I'd do with it, but, *ahhh…*" Justin reached out and gripped Patsy's hand.

Nudging him fiercely with her elbow, Patsy's pained expression held warning. She was going to kill him when she got him alone.

He bit his lip. "Uh, without an actual exam…*ahhh,*" he stammered.

Knowing him as well as she did, Patsy could tell he was biting back a belly laugh. She could also tell he had just seen the green flag and, unable to control himself, was off to the proverbial races. She rolled her eyes. Great. They were really getting off onto the right foot here. She couldn't wait for tomorrow night.

"Just off the cuff I'd probably recommend having it removed."

Grace gasped. "The whole breast?"

"No, no, no." Justin chuckled, a deep, doctorlike chuckle. "Just, ah, that little…ah, spot." Averting his eyes, he gestured to the nebulous area between her waist and her collarbone.

Moving forward, Brenda tapped him on the arm. "Since you're passing out advice," she teased, "what do you think of my nose?" she asked, presenting her profile to him. "What would you do about that?" She pointed to a small bump that Patsy had always thought had given her pretty face character.

Justin gleefully ignored Patsy's heel as she dug it into his foot. Directing his gaze at Brenda, he tapped his lip and assumed his practiced Dr. Oscar frown. "What do you smell?" he demanded as he reached out and, taking her wrist, felt for her pulse.

"Right now?" she asked, surprised.

"Yes." Dropping her wrist, he felt her forehead with the back of his hand.

"Um, food from the buffet table." The corners of her

mouth curved down in contemplation. "And, um, perfume and let's see…" She smiled up at Justin. "Your after-shave."

"Say ahh," he commanded.

A quixotic glaze filled her eyes. *"Ahhhhh,"* she breathed.

"Very good," Justin said. He peered into her mouth and nodded in a scholarly fashion, then patted the back of her hand. "That's precisely right. Your nose seems to work just fine. I wouldn't do a thing to it. It's very attractive, just the way it is."

Patsy grimaced. He was enjoying himself a tad too much. What would he do if someone demanded a business card? Or an appointment for a consultation? Or even worse, what if someone had a medical emergency, and they needed a doctor? Although, she thought relaxing slightly, chances were no one would need an emergency face-lift tonight. But still. He shouldn't ham it up quite so much.

She had to admit as she stood back watching him play his part with such easy humor, she could almost believe he knew what he was talking about. Cool as a cucumber. She couldn't help but smile, as he straightened his jacket and winked over at her.

"Thank you, Dr. Oscar." Brenda bubbled, beaming.

"It's nothing." His curt and professional, yet suave and sexy, reply was reminiscent of George Clooney's bedside manner on TV.

"Dr. Oscar!" Joyce called, elbowing Grace and Brenda out of her way. "I was wondering if you wouldn't mind having a little look at this…" she muttered, and reaching down, hiked the skirt of her voluminous velvet gown up to her knee.

Bitsy pushed between them, happy to sacrifice herself to act as a human shield. "Later, Joyce," she said breezily.

"Dr. Oscar still has more rounds to make." Her laughter tinkled as she steered him away from the group.

Taking Bitsy at her word, Justin rose above and beyond the call of duty, even by Marcus Welby's standards, and proceeded to make the rounds among the reunion attendees, recommending a nip here, a tuck there, and a smattering of hair plugs for everyone. The shallow waters were fine and Justin had leapt in with both wing tips and was swimming gleefully with the sharks. Patsy, gamely trying to keep up with his kooky curveballs, finally had to throw up her hands in futility and let him have his fun.

"Come say hello to Mrs. Renfru. She's been waiting for you," Bitsy invited after they'd spoken to, and given medical advice to nearly everyone in the room.

Looking across the gym at the wrenching sight, Patsy saw Mrs. Renfru's darling little time-weathered face smiling brightly up at her from her seat in a wheelchair, and felt a stab of shame. Licking her lips, she glanced up at Justin, and wished that she could disappear.

Surely Mrs. Renfru could see that, even from across the darkened gymnasium. Patsy swallowed hard and wondered if perhaps she should throw herself on Mrs. Renfru's mercy, and tell her the truth.

Feebly returning Mrs. Renfru's sunny smile, Patsy changed her mind. No. She simply couldn't bring herself to disappoint her wonderful dance teacher.

"Mrs. Renfru. How wonderful to see you." Patsy smiled, as she approached.

Bitsy moved off to speak with another group of alumni, leaving the three of them alone in the corner near the bleachers. Teacher and student hugged tenderly.

"Hello, Patsy, my darling girl. Please…" Mrs. Renfru gestured a fluttery hand toward the bench near her wheelchair. "Won't you and your young man sit for a moment?" She touched her short, silvery curls, and adjusted her heavily rimmed glasses to rest more comfortably against her plump cheeks. Her long, heavy gold earrings dangled and swayed as she spoke.

"Yes," Patsy murmured, smiling gently at the teacher who could still play her like a violin. No one was dearer than Mrs. Renfru.

"I would love to get up on the stage and dance with you tomorrow, however I fell last month, and broke my hip. I'll be having surgery soon, but for now, my chair makes life so much easier."

"Bitsy mentioned that you'd had an accident."

"Just a little spill while playing the *premiere danseuse*," the elderly woman trilled in theatrical fashion. "But enough about me. I was simply delighted to discover that you had soared to such heights in your career as a dancer." Extending a delicate, shaky hand, she clasped Justin by the arm and winked. "You will forgive an old woman her silly puns."

"No," Justin teased, "but, I'll forgive a beautiful woman."

"Ah, Patsy." Mrs. Renfru hummed her mirth and batted her eyes. "Yes, my darling girl, you've done exceedingly well for yourself, I see."

"Yes," Patsy agreed, taking her old dance teacher's frail hand in her own. The skin was as thin as paper and clung loosely to her arthritic fingers. To Patsy, however, this hand was not old at all, but was instead the strong hand that had guided her through many trying times in her youth. She felt tears well in her eyes.

"Patsy, as Bitsy no doubt told you, I'm so very proud of all your wonderful accomplishments."

Patsy shot Justin a heartsick glance. "Oh, no," she demurred.

Oblivious to Patsy's discomfort, she continued. "All in just ten short years. Simply amazing. My darling girl, you were and continue to be, the joy of my career.'' To Justin she said, ''Patsy was one of the brightest, most caring, delightful pupils I'd ever had the pleasure to teach. Seeing you dance tomorrow night will be the highlight of my career.''

Justin glanced at Patsy then to his shoes then back to Patsy.

Rendered momentarily speechless, Patsy's mind reeled as she stared hopelessly at Justin. His face reflected the guilt she felt. This was terrible. She didn't want to lie to this woman. She didn't want to lie to anybody. It was all a joke. A big, dumb practical joke.

''My darling girl, if you will forgive me, now that I've seen you, I shall be on my way.'' She winked confidentially at Patsy. ''I find this type of thing tiring, to say the least. But, it was worth it to see your lovely face once again. Ten years is simply too long to go. Come give us a hug.''

''Oh, Mrs. Renfru,'' Patsy whispered around the giant lump that had lodged in her throat. ''It was so good to see you again, too.''

The grand old lady hugged first Patsy, then her husband, and with a cheery wave, set her wheelchair into motion and bid them good-night.

Chapter Ten

Justin turned from his moonlit view of the little creek for which Patsy's high school was named, and watched as she silently joined him on the balcony that was just outside the sliding door of their adjoining hotel rooms. Being that he was sharing a room with the boys and she with the girls, the balcony was the only place where they could discuss the evening's events without disturbing the now slumbering kids.

After what seemed like an endless day, they were finally alone. The night sky was cloudless, and stars, like a carpet of diamonds, twinkled down at them where they stood. Patsy was still wearing her sequined dress, but she'd taken her hair down and brushed out the hair spray. She was so incredibly beautiful. Inside and out.

Justin studied her, his heart heavy with guilt and shame over his misbehavior tonight. He knew he owed her an apology, and was trying to form the words in his mind as she floated through the shadows to his side.

Looking down into her beautiful face, his heart skipped a beat, as he tried to sort his myriad emotions.

He wasn't sure what, exactly had gotten into him. Perhaps it had been a little rebellion against a room full of Darlenes. Perhaps it had been the exhilaration of having everyone look at him with such awe. Such respect. Perhaps it had simply been a little streak of the devil coming out in him. Whatever the reason, he knew that when it came to this evening, he'd gone more than a little overboard.

And, while it had been more fun than a barrel of monkeys, it had been wrong. Sweet little old Mrs. Renfru had brought that home with startling clarity. While these people might be out of his league socially speaking, they were still people with feelings. The fact that they had money, power and position didn't make them any less so. He'd made horses' patoots out of most of them without half trying, and he was ashamed of himself.

Yeah, he thought, reaching up and rubbing the knots at the back of his neck, this whole charade was as much his fault—if not more—as Patsy's, and he had no one to blame for this deception but himself.

Patsy had wanted to tell the truth a long time ago. It was he who had botched her efforts.

Well, it was time to come clean. They should tell the truth. First thing tomorrow morning. It was the only way. As he looked down into Patsy's sweet, guileless face, he knew that she would see it that way, too. It was one of the things he loved about her. She cared about these people, regardless of their class distinction.

She would be glad that he was going to support her in the truth. That settled in his mind, he smiled at her.

"How'd you get the twins to go to bed?" she wondered in a whisper.

"Threatened bodily harm." He leaned toward her. "Of course they were somewhat contrite after the scene with Bitsy's husband."

Patsy moaned. "Don't remind me. I still can't believe they actually stole his wallet."

"Well, at least this time, they gave it back," he said, wearily.

"True. And, I'd have to say, for me anyway, the mortification of that little episode paled in comparison to discovering that I was wearing one of Bitsy's cast-offs."

Justin arched a brow. "I don't know. I think you looked pretty stricken when the mechanic came in and announced that your car was fixed and he'd parked it and the U-Haul right outside the big glass gym doors under the big bright street lamp."

Patsy moaned. "Well, for pity's sake. You'd think none of them had ever seen a twenty-five-year-old station wagon before." With a light sigh, she shook her head.

Stretching, he came over to lean against the wrought-iron railing with her. "Tired?"

He ran a light finger across her cheek, leaving a trail of fire in its wake. Her breath caught in her throat as she looked up at him and nodded mutely.

"Me, too."

The rich timbre of his voice mixed with the night sounds created a restlessness in Patsy. No matter how she tried to fight it, something about Justin aroused her as no other man ever had. He was everything she'd ever wanted in a man— and more. She cast an appreciative eye over his handsome face. These extraordinary good looks were the "and more" part, she guessed, remembering how that dimple in his chin used to annoy her. Now, it seemed, she was always fighting the absurd impulse to press her lips to that spot.

Pushing her thumbs into the cool metal of the railing, she ran them back and forth and angled her head at him. "I couldn't believe the way some of my old girlfriends followed you around, begging for suggestions on how they could improve their looks."

He winced and cast her a penitent glance.

"Don't worry." She chuckled. "They loved the free advice."

"Patsy, I'm not qualified to give medical advice." Sober faced, he looked at her, and ran a hand over his shadowed cheeks and chin. "I went too far tonight."

"Well, maybe a little, but it was all in good fun."

"Was it?"

Squinting at him, Patsy wondered what was going through his mind, but at that moment she was simply too exhausted and filled with anxiety about tomorrow to delve into more than superficial matters.

"You know," she sighed, "they haven't changed a bit."

"None of them?"

"No."

Justin shrugged out of his jacket, draped it over her bare shoulders and then proceeded to loosen his tie. "Not even you?" he asked as he rolled the sleeves of his white shirt up to his elbows.

She shivered as the warmth of his jacket permeated her body. "I want to believe I have."

Leaning against the railing on his forearms, his hands dangled over the edge as he studied her. In the pale moonlight, she could see the pensive lines etched at the corners of his eyes.

"I want to believe that, too."

"Why?" Her heart began to pound. Something was wrong. She could tell.

"Because, a long time ago, I knew someone… Someone who reminded me of—" Justin's gaze glittered through the darkness and his sigh was heavy "—them."

The muscles in his jaw worked and it was obvious that he had something on his mind. Turning, Patsy watched the various night lights shimmer on the silver thread that was

Willow Creek. He was referring to her. He must be. He thought she was still one of them.

"Oh," she murmured, feeling suddenly despondent.

As if he sensed her angst, Justin braced himself on his hip against the railing and pulled her into his arms.

"Patsy," he said, his voice rumbling comfortingly beneath her ear, slightly gruff with emotion.

"Yes?" she whispered around the lump that filled her throat.

"You don't have to go through with it."

"With what?"

"Putting on a show for those phonies."

"What would you have me do?"

"You could always tell them the truth. Now."

It took a beat for this to register to the recesses of her sluggish brain.

"Now?" she gasped, rearing back and looking up at him, agog.

"Well, not now. Tomorrow would be soon enough."

"Have you lost your *mind?* It's a little late in the game for that, don't you think?" She blinked up at him, trying to ascertain if he was serious. "And what about Mrs. Renfru?"

"I have a feeling she, of all people, would understand. In fact, after meeting her, I...I don't know...I just think she should know."

"Oh, Justin! No! No, I couldn't disappoint her that way." She gave her head a vehement shake. "Or the kids."

He arched a sardonic brow. "Are you sure you're worried about Mrs. Renfru and the kids? Or is it your reputation as the girl most likely to succeed that makes you want to carry on with this ludicrous charade?"

"Ludicrous?" Patsy gasped, then looking over her shoulder into the girls' room, lowered her voice. Angrily

she shook off his embrace. "You're *serious!* You want me to pull out of the show at the last minute!"

He shrugged. "It was just a thought."

"I can't believe you!" Whether from lack of sleep, or nerves, or the look of disguised censure behind his sexy eyes, she couldn't be sure, but suddenly, Patsy was furious. "After all the work those kids have gone to? After we've just spent an evening conning my entire graduating class..."

Justin's eyes slid closed, and he exhaled long and hard. "I'm not proud of what we did back there tonight, if that's what you're implying."

"What?" she snapped. "How could you do this to me? How could you undermine my confidence the night before I have to go out there and dance in front of nearly five hundred people?"

"I don't know." His sigh was weary. "I'm sorry. I guess I thought I knew you better than I do."

"What the hell is that supposed to mean?" Patsy demanded, pushing her hair out of her face and over her shoulder with furious hands. "You know me just fine. Better than anyone has ever known me in my life."

Suffering from exhaustion himself, Justin snapped. "Well, then, I guess I thought that the woman I knew— when we got here, and saw how ridiculous this whole situation was—would come to her senses."

Tears of anger and frustration brimmed in her eyes. *Why was he doing this to her?* "So," she sniffed, "now, I've lost my senses?"

"I don't know. Have you?" He sighed, clearly frustrated at the way their communication had broken down. "Don't you even feel a little bit remorseful that we were lying to everyone all evening?"

Patsy's jaw dropped. "Forgive me, Dr. Oscar, if my

memory seems a little fuzzy, but I believe you were the one writing prescriptions on cocktail napkins all evening.''

"And I regret it."

"Oh, sure!"

"Don't you get it?'' Justin's whisper was growing ever louder as he gripped the railing and leaned over her. His words were rapid with the heat of his thoughts. "You were by far the most successful woman in that entire room tonight. Would any of them give the time of day to a homeless kid, the way you have? Would any of them move out from under their inheritance and scrape together a living the way you have? Would any of them give up everything they hold so dear and dedicate their lives to helping others?''

Patsy simply stared at him, her mouth gaping.

Firmly in place on his soapbox, Justin continued, his tone vehement. "Yet, for some mind-boggling reason, you still seem to insist on feeling like you have something to prove to those snobs.''

"No... I...'' she stammered weakly, her head spinning. *That couldn't be right.*

"I thought I was really beginning to know you. But, I can see that I was wrong. Maybe you haven't changed all that much after all.'' He looked at her and gave his head a shake, his smile self-deprecating. "You know—'' his laughter rang hollow ''—this is good. I'm finally realizing that you and I are from different worlds. I need to get it through my thick head that I can't play out of my league.''

Patsy, her lifeless heart now breaking in two, watched as he stared at her for a long while, seeming to see her as some kind of ghost of girlfriend past. Well, she wasn't Darcy or Dora or Darlene, or whatever the heck Holly had said her name was. She didn't like being compared to someone she'd only heard about through the grapevine. It wasn't fair.

Where was her Justin?

The compassionate, supportive man that had stood beside her that evening, through the craziest, most disgusting night of her life. Okay, so he'd been a little over the top, but hey, he'd been there when it had counted.

Okay, okay. So a nagging little voice in the back of her head suggested he might be right. Perhaps she, too, felt a little slimy after having lied to so many people that evening. Especially someone as sweet as Mrs. Renfru. But this was a hell of a time for him to get a conscience, she thought, fuming, angry with him.

Angry with herself.

"I need some sleep," she snapped, ripping his jacket off her shoulders and thrusting it into his chest.

"I can see that," he agreed sharply and, turning on his heel, strode across the balcony to his own sliding glass door, and closing it none too gently, disappeared for the night.

Angrily swiping away a tear, Patsy sagged against the railing, and wondered what she'd ever seen in a pigheaded man that was second only to her father when it came to being completely and utterly exasperating.

The following day flew by in a blur for Patsy. Aside from the few curt remarks they passed between them, contact between her and Justin was practically nil. The strain between them made Patsy want to break down and sob. But she didn't have time to sit around and feel sorry for herself. She'd had a "classmates only" brunch that Saturday morning, and after that, a rehearsal in the gym with the kids and the orchestra, that did not go well at all.

However, Patsy knew from her own recital experience that the dress rehearsal before any performance was usually a disaster. She only hoped that her little troupe could somehow perform a miracle before they were laughed off the stage.

By the time seven o'clock rolled around that evening, the kids were all dressed in their costumes, hair neatly combed, lips and cheeks reddened with stage makeup. As they were scheduled to go on any minute now, the kids were waiting in the wings with her, fairly giddy with nervous excitement. Patsy only hoped she didn't throw up before one of the kids did.

Already, several fabulously talented, and Patsy could only guess, very expensive warm-up type musical acts had hit the stage, and been received with enthusiastic applause. However, this did nothing to calm the nervously flitting butterflies that had taken up residence in her stomach.

All day long, Justin's words had haunted her.

She hadn't had a minute alone with him to find out if he never wanted to see her again after this weekend. Her stomach constricted painfully at the dismal thought and she blinked back the tears that threatened. However, in a way she was glad they hadn't had a chance to speak in private. If her heart was going to be shattered, she'd rather wait until after this performance. It had enough problems without her sobbing through the entire routine.

As she glanced around the backstage area, she saw Justin across the proscenium watching them from the wings opposite hers. Her heart clutched as their gazes collided. He looked as haggard as she felt.

Why was she doing this again? she wondered, filled with nervous questions that spun in her head until she feared she might faint. Justin was right. Her motives were all wrong. Unfortunately, before she could puzzle out what she should do about it, Bitsy was at the microphone, introducing her and the kids to her former classmates.

The lights went out and she walked out on stage, the way she had rehearsed with the kids all afternoon. Once they were all in place, the lights flashed on, and Patsy looked out over the audience.

And, she saw.

Patsy Brubaker suddenly saw what she'd been blinded to her entire life, until this very moment.

The bored expressions. The expensive furs. The clothes. The jewelry that cost more than it would take to feed for a year one of the parentless children that stood in their cheap costumes and new tap shoes so bravely at her side. And, the incongruity of it all disgusted her. While she was disgusted with the unfair situation that life had handed the Miracle House children, she was far more disgusted with herself. More disgusted than Justin ever thought of being.

She was moving heaven and earth to impress these people. To fake them into thinking that she was successful on their terms.

She didn't want to be successful on their terms. Patsy Brubaker suddenly realized that she wanted to be successful on her terms. On God's terms. On Big Daddy's terms.

And, on Justin's terms.

As the orchestra struck up their number—and her cue to begin dancing came and went—Patsy stood rooted to her spot and, tilting her chin, looked to Justin for support. Lifting a hand, she silenced the orchestra and took a deep breath.

Puzzled, the kids exchanged fearful glances and shuffled nervously at her side. From her spot in the wings, Gayle clutched the wall and slid into a chair, her eyes wide with worry.

As Patsy looked out over the audience, she suddenly realized that Justin had been right all along. She may not have the fancy clothes and cars anymore, but, she thought, glancing at the freshly scrubbed, freckled faces that stood behind her, she had treasures that most of these people could never comprehend. Her eyes strayed once again to Justin.

An uneasy hush fell over the audience, and Patsy knew, as her gaze met and merged with Justin's, that she had to say her piece. As she moved to Bitsy's microphone, she knew it was time to tell the truth.

Chapter Eleven

"Ten years ago, you voted me the girl most likely to succeed," Patsy began, her voice quavering with a curious mixture of fear and purpose. Slowly casting her gaze around the room, she smiled ruefully. "Well—" her deep exhalation puffed her cheeks slightly "—the truth of the matter is, I have not only *not* succeeded in any of the ways that we expected I would." She smiled at the murmuring that rippled across the audience, and bravely continued. "But I view tonight as my biggest failure to date."

Reaching next to her, she grabbed Charlyn and Patrick's hands, to reassure them and to steady herself.

"You, uh, see, I'm trying to learn from my mistakes these days, and that's why I have to tell you the truth."

The audience looked around, puzzled, and resumed murmuring amongst themselves.

"I lied. I don't know how I can put it any more simply than that. I lied to all of you, and urged other people that I care about—" she pulled the kids close, then shot a meaningful glance into the wings at Justin "—very deeply, to join me in my debacle.

"I could tell you that I lied for a good purpose. Or because I didn't want to let anyone down. Or because there had been some mistakes in my communications with Bitsy. But that doesn't excuse the truth of the matter, and that is that I lied to you all because I wanted to impress you."

A hush fell over the crowd as they leaned forward, straining to hear every word. Justin moved to the edge of the stage, and smiled his encouragement at her. Fortified by the love and pride she saw burning in his eyes, she continued.

"You see, in the ten years since I have graduated from high school, I have not gotten my college degree, I have not married, I have not had any children, nor do I have an upwardly mobile career." She sighed. "I don't own enough clothes to fill a suitcase, and I live in a trailer on the children's ranch where I work. You've seen my car. I'm making payments on the U-Haul rental."

A ripple of laughter rolled across the audience.

"Many of you would probably say I've failed, in the ten years since I graduated from high school. And, until about four months ago, I would be hard-pressed to disagree with you."

Tears sprang unbidden into Patsy's eyes as an emotional tidal wave rolled over her. Looking out into the sea of faces that made up her graduating class, Patsy suddenly knew that she could well and truly kiss the old Patsy Brubaker goodbye. That person no longer existed. In her place, stood a woman whose hopes and dreams had nothing to do with wealth or prestige, and everything to do with love.

She was more her father's daughter than she ever would have imagined possible.

Taking a deep, cleansing breath, Patsy smiled at the crowd, as they sat agog, staring with arched brows and slack jaws.

"I've had a lot of failures since I left these hallowed halls," Patsy continued. "A lot of disappointment. In myself, mostly. But, I've learned a lot from my experiences. And I think I can tell you what success means to me now.''

She pulled Charlyn and Patrick close and gestured to the other children to gather around.

''For the last four months, I have worked for my brother Buck and his wife, Holly. They are the cofounders of the Miracle House Ranch, a shelter for homeless children. Right now, they are in the process of building the permanent housing structures on the ranch land they own, and hope someday to be able to house over a hundred children. It's a slow process, and since none of us are rich anymore, we have to get our money the old-fashioned way. We have to earn it.''

Another ripple of laughter.

''Since I have worked with these wonderful children, my ideas of success have changed from dreaming my way through dance class in Europe, to hearing the laughter of a healthy baby. To seeing a teenager learning to love and be loved for the first time in her life. Watching orphaned kids finding moms and dads to adopt them and give them permanent homes.''

Some sniffles could be heard from the rapt audience as Patsy continued to regale them with tales of her children. Her life. Her sense of self-worth. The laughter. The hope. The love.

Justin, his eyes shining with pride, quietly walked out onto the stage and stood by her as she talked. Without breaking her impassioned speech, she reached out and took his hand and squeezed. And he squeezed back.

''Perhaps this is not the world's view of success,'' she told the attentive class, ''but it's mine now. I've never been happier in my life. It's true,'' she mused. ''Money does not buy happiness. But,'' she added with a twinkle in her eye, ''it can buy a lot of supplies.

''I know a lot of you have been very blessed materially

all your lives and are looking for a way to give. If that's the case, I urge you to think about Miracle House. Give of your money. Your time. Yourselves. You won't regret it.''

As she painted loving portraits of some of the children she had come to know and love, men, women and children alike sat glued to their seats, soaking up her every word.

''Nothing is more priceless than seeing a child succeed in an otherwise hopeless situation. I invite you all to take a little time and come visit us at Miracle House. Come on and meet the kids. Maybe you, too, will fall in love.''

Justin's arm slowly circled her waist and pulled her close.

''I'm so sorry I lied to you all.'' She looked up at Justin. ''We both are.''

He nodded.

''I wanted so badly to be somebody in your eyes. But, I guess I've learned one important lesson, and that is that I need to be somebody in my own eyes. I know I'm not the most successful one in our graduating class by a long shot, but I wouldn't trade my life for anything.''

When she was finished, there wasn't a dry eye in the house. From her seat in the front row, Mrs. Renfru began to clap. The audience joined in, and soon the applause became thunderous with shouts and whistles of approval. The band began to play, the lights dimmed and, grinning broadly, the children began to move into their much rehearsed formation. Justin moved off to the side of the stage, nodding his encouragement. Something magic was in the air as what had been a bedraggled, uncoordinated group of ragamuffins suddenly came to life as a polished dance troupe. Blinking away her tears, Patsy smiled at the animated faces behind her and fell into step.

When they had finished, without so much as a single mistake, Patsy bowed, then turning, clapped for the kids.

Then, arms around each other, joined by Justin, they all left the stage.

Bitsy trotted up to the microphone and suggested that the bleachers be pushed back against the wall to make way for a dance floor. The orchestra had agreed to stay and donate their time for a dance-a-thon. A dollar a dance into the wee hours, with the proceeds going to Miracle House Ranch.

Backstage, the kids begged to go help set up the dance floor. Waving them away with a few instructions to behave themselves, Justin pulled Patsy into a darkened corner where they could be alone. From where they stood, the sounds of a party in the early stages wafted back to them.

"I owe you an apology," Justin said, taking her hands in his.

Patsy shook her head then let it fall against his chest. "No. No, I'm the one who should apologize for getting you into this mess in the first place."

Tilting her chin up with his thumb and forefinger, he looked deeply into her eyes. "I'm sorry," he murmured, and the emotion of his entire heart was packed in the two little words.

"Me, too," she whispered back.

"I was unfairly comparing you to someone I used to know." He shrugged and pulled her into his arms. "I was afraid."

"Of what?"

"Of making a mistake again. Of getting hurt. Of hurting you."

"Are you afraid anymore?"

Eyes flashing, he gently cupped her face in his hands and lightly kissed her lips. "No."

"Why?" she whispered, her heart leaping into her throat at the look of raw, smoldering possession she saw in his eyes.

"Because *you* are the woman I fell in love with. Not the girl who was once voted most likely to succeed."

"I am this woman, when I'm with you." The tears that had threatened for so long finally began to spill joyously down her cheeks. *He loved her!* And she knew without a single doubt that she loved him, too.

"Then, I suppose that means you are going to have to be with me for a long, long time."

"How long?"

"How does forever sound to you?"

Patsy sighed, knowing in her heart that she had just exceeded Big Daddy's wildest dreams of success for his only daughter.

"It sounds," she murmured against his searching lips, "a little bit like heaven."

Epilogue

Five years later

"**I** still don't know why you didn't just fill in the truth on *this* questionnaire," Justin sighed, as he steered his family over to a shaded picnic table near the Willow Creek High School waterfront, and began passing out cans of Coke. "Didn't you learn anything from our last reunion experience? After all, what's wrong with the plain and simple truth?"

Patsy looked over her shoulder to see if the twins were following. "Nothing, honey. It's just that my classmates already all know the truth and it's not all that interesting to most of them anymore. And, as you well know, I was voted..."

"The Girl Most Likely To Succeed," her growing family chorused. Mikey and Marky rolled their eyes. "We know, we know."

Patsy grinned and, shifting the baby she'd had with Justin up onto her shoulder, patted his back. Following in the

Brubaker family tradition, they'd named their little son Travis, for Randy Travis and Travis Tritt. She glanced up at one of the twins. "Mikey, honey, get me a bottle out of the diaper bag, will you?"

"Sure, Mom," came the prompt and courteous reply.

Justin pulled their four-year-old daughter Crystal Gayle onto his lap and rested his chin on the russet curls that were so like her birth-mother, Gayle's.

"Criminy, Patsy, I don't even know what an oboe looks like, let alone how to play one for the Philharmonic."

Patsy giggled. "I know, but you think so fast on your feet. I just loved it when that noisy rock band Bitsy had hired asked you to sit in with them for a number last night. You were very good. Grace, Brenda and Joyce were really rocking."

Justin snorted. "Yeah right. Luckily, I'm not the only one in that band who can't read music."

"Besides," Patsy continued after she'd finished laughing, "I don't know why you're complaining. It's not like I know anything about producing major motion pictures for Hollywood."

"Fine, but at the twenty-year reunion, if you're going to tell a whopper, tell one that doesn't make me look like an idiot, for once."

"Okay, I'll try to stick closer to the truth."

"Good."

"Actually, the truth is my favorite," Patsy sighed contentedly, and taking the bottle from Mikey, popped it into baby Travis's mouth. Five years ago, we didn't have anything, and now look at us. We have four fabulous children, a lovely house on the hill next to Buck and Holly, their beautiful daughter, LeAnn and her baby brother, Clint, and an ever-growing Miracle Ranch, filled with love and laughter."

"And each other," Justin said, smiling indulgently at her.

Patsy reached out and squeezed his hand. He squeezed back.

With a glance around the picnic area at the group that made up her graduating class, Patsy sighed, "I suppose we should mingle." She lifted a questioning brow at her husband.

"I'd rather sneak back behind the bleachers and neck..." Justin grinned hopefully at his wife of five wonderful years.

"Dr. Oscar," Patsy whispered over their baby boy's head, "I thought you'd never ask."

* * * * *

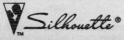

Take 2 bestselling love stories FREE

Plus get a FREE surprise gift!

Special Limited-Time Offer

Mail to Silhouette Reader Service™

> 3010 Walden Avenue
> P.O. Box 1867
> Buffalo, N.Y. 14240-1867

YES! Please send me 2 free Silhouette Romance™ novels and my free surprise gift. Then send me 6 brand-new novels every month, which I will receive months before they appear in bookstores. Bill me at the low price of $2.90 each plus 25¢ delivery and applicable sales tax, if any.* That's the complete price, and a saving of over 10% off the cover prices—quite a bargain! I understand that accepting the books and gift places me under no obligation ever to buy any books. I can always return a shipment and cancel at any time. Even if I never buy another book from Silhouette, the 2 free books and the surprise gift are mine to keep forever.

215 SEN CH7S

Name	(PLEASE PRINT)	
Address	Apt. No.	
City	State	Zip

This offer is limited to one order per household and not valid to present Silhouette Romance™ subscribers. *Terms and prices are subject to change without notice. Sales tax applicable in N.Y.

USROM-98　　　　　　　　　　　　　　　　　©1990 Harlequin Enterprises Limited

For a limited time, Harlequin and Silhouette have an offer you just can't refuse.

In November and December 1998:

BUY **ANY** TWO HARLEQUIN
OR SILHOUETTE BOOKS and
SAVE $10.00
off future purchases

OR BUY ANY THREE HARLEQUIN OR SILHOUETTE BOOKS
AND **SAVE $20.00** OFF FUTURE PURCHASES!

(each coupon is good for $1.00 off the purchase of two
Harlequin or Silhouette books)

···

JUST BUY 2 HARLEQUIN OR SILHOUETTE BOOKS, SEND US YOUR
NAME, ADDRESS AND 2 PROOFS OF PURCHASE (CASH REGISTER
RECEIPTS) AND HARLEQUIN WILL SEND YOU A COUPON BOOKLET
WORTH $10.00 OFF FUTURE PURCHASES OF HARLEQUIN OR
SILHOUETTE BOOKS IN 1999. SEND US 3 PROOFS OF PURCHASE AND
WE WILL SEND YOU 2 COUPON BOOKLETS WITH A TOTAL SAVING OF
$20.00. (ALLOW 4-6 WEEKS DELIVERY) OFFER EXPIRES
DECEMBER 31, 1998.

···

I accept your offer! Please send me a coupon booklet(s), to:

NAME: _____

ADDRESS: _____

CITY: _____ STATE/PROV.: _____ POSTAL/ZIP CODE: _____

Send your name and address, along with your cash register
receipts for proofs of purchase, to:

In the U.S.	In Canada
Harlequin Books	Harlequin Books
P.O. Box 9057	P.O. Box 622
Buffalo, NY	Fort Erie, Ontario
14269	L2A 5X3

PHQ4982

THESE BACHELOR DADS NEED A LITTLE TENDERNESS—AND A WHOLE LOT OF LOVING!

**January 1999—A Rugged Ranchin' Dad
by Kia Cochrane (SR# 1343)**
Tragedy had wedged Stone Tyler's family apart. Now this rugged rancher would do everything in his power to be the perfect daddy—and recapture his wife's heart—before time ran out....

**April 1999 — Prince Charming's Return
by Myrna Mackenzie (SR# 1361)**
Gray Alexander was back in town—and had just met the son he had never known he had. Now he wanted to make Cassie Pratt pay for her deception eleven years ago...even if the price was marriage!

And in **June 1999** don't miss Donna Clayton's touching story of Dylan Minster, a man who has been raising his daughter all alone....

Fall in love with our FABULOUS FATHERS!

And look for more FABULOUS FATHERS in the months to come. Only from

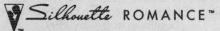 ROMANCE™

Available wherever Silhouette books are sold.

Look us up on-line at: http://www.romance.net   SRFFJ-J

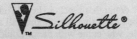

COMING NEXT MONTH

#1342 THE BOSS AND THE BEAUTY —Donna Clayton
Loving the Boss

Cindy Cooper dreamed of marrying her boss, even though she doubted handsome executive Kyle Prentice would look twice at a plain Jane like her. But when Cindy's true beauty was revealed, could she trust that Kyle's sudden attraction was more than skin-deep?

#1343 A RUGGED RANCHIN' DAD—Kia Cochrane
Fabulous Fathers

Stone Tyler loved his wife and his son, but tragedy had divided his family. Now this rugged rancher would do everything in his power to be the perfect daddy—and recapture his wife's heart—before time ran out....

#1344 MARRY ME, KATE—Judy Christenberry
The Lucky Charm Sisters

He needed to prevent his mother from pushing him up the aisle. She needed money to rebuild her father's dream. So William Hardison and Kate O'Connor struck a bargain. They'd marry for one year, and their problems would be solved. It was the perfect marriage—until a little thing called love complicated the deal....

#1345 GRANTED: A FAMILY FOR BABY—Carol Grace
Best-Kept Wishes

All Suzy Fenton wanted was a daddy for her sweet son. But sexy sheriff Brady Wilson thought his able secretary was looking for Mr. Right in all the wrong places. And that maybe, just maybe, her future husband was right before her eyes....

#1346 THE MILLION-DOLLAR COWBOY—Martha Shields
Cowboys to the Rescue

She didn't like cowboys, but rodeo champion Travis Eden made Becca Lawson's pulse race. Maybe it was because they had grown up together or because Travis was unlike any cowboy she had ever met. Or maybe it was purely a matter of the heart....

#1347 FAMILY BY THE BUNCH—Amy Frazier
Family Matters

There was never any doubt that rancher Hank Whittaker wanted a family—he just wasn't expecting five children all at once! Or beautiful Nessa Little, who came with them. Could Nessa convince the lone cowboy to take this ready-made family into his heart?